'I couldn't wa[...]

Olivia looked up a[...]
'I've waited long e[...]
single second more.'

Tony couldn't believe what he was hearing.
Olivia wanted him, and he wanted *her* as much as
he'd ever wanted anything in his life. His hand
shook as he reached for her and pulled her into
the house.

Suddenly he realized she was staring down at his
body. He'd forgotten that when he'd jerked the
door open he wasn't even close to being dressed.
Her gaze rested on his blatant arousal clearly
visible beneath his soft cotton boxers.

She began unbuttoning her coat, and as each
button slid free, his heartbeat accelerated. First he
saw soft pale flesh, the gentle swells of her
breasts. As the coat parted farther he saw that she
was nearly naked, covered only by the teddy he'd
admired the day before in her shop.

In that moment he knew they wouldn't even make
it as far as the bedroom.

Dear Reader,

Can you still remember your first kiss, your first sexual touch, the first time you made love? The memory or imagery of lovemaking, the scents, the sights and sounds of being totally connected to another human being in such a basic way is an unforgettable experience!

That's why I want my heroes to be men who are sexually greedy, who wallow in a woman's soft moans of pleasure. And I want heroines who aren't ashamed to be women, to give and take every measure of pleasure imaginable with a man they love.

Which is why I'm so glad BLAZE has been created for Temptation®. Writing a BLAZE offers me freedom as a writer to explore all the faces of love and romance, with all the realism of a modern relationship between two intelligent, sensual adults.

I sincerely hope you enjoy my efforts, and I look forward to hearing from you.

Lori Foster

You can reach Lori at Harlequin Mills & Boon Ltd, Eton House, 18-24 Paradise Road, Richmond, Surrey TW9 1SR.

It's hot...and it's out of control.
Don't miss the next red-hot reads from
Temptation's BLAZE:

Night Rhythms by Elda Minger (September 1998)
Fantasy by Lori Foster (October 1998)

SCANDALIZED!

by

Lori Foster

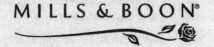
MILLS & BOON®

*MILLS & BOON and MILLS & BOON with the Rose Device
are registered trademarks of the publisher.
TEMPTATION is a registered trademark of
Harlequin Enterprises Limited, used under licence.*

*First published in Great Britain 1998
by Harlequin Mills & Boon Limited,
Eton House, 18-24 Paradise Road, Richmond, Surrey TW9 1SR*

© Lori Foster 1997

ISBN 0 263 81185 9

With much gratitude to Anita Gunnufson for all her
medical assistance in this book. I really enjoyed our
long-distance chats.

And to Glenn Davis. I love you, Dad.

21-9807

*Printed and bound in Great Britain
by Caledonian International Book Manufacturing Ltd, Glasgow*

1

SHE WAS THE PERFECT WOMAN to have his baby.

Tony Austin continued to stare, analyzing her features, considering the construction of her body. He'd already done so, of course, but now he was more thorough. She wasn't beautiful, but that was okay, because beauty wasn't essential to his plan. And she *was* striking, even arresting in her presence, her confidence and poise.

Though he tried to stop himself, his gaze was repeatedly drawn to her, and finally Olivia Anderson caught him looking. The small, curious smile she sent him took his breath away, but he shook his head, deciding his reaction was excitement for his plan and nothing else.

That was all it could be.

As always, she looked elegant. She wore a simple black dress and black heels, but that had little to do with his heightened interest. He had made a decision, and she was deeply involved in that decision whether she knew it yet or not. He rubbed his hands together, feeling his anticipation build.

He'd been acquainted with her for three years now as a business associate, and he knew she'd only at-

tended his party as a means of furthering that association. Nothing in their relationship was of a personal
nature—and he intended to keep it that way.

Just two days ago, she'd presented him with a proposal to expand her business that would add one more
of her novelty lingerie shops to another Austin Crown
hotel. He hadn't given her an answer yet, but he
would. Tonight. And then he'd have a question of his
own to present.

For the first time in a very long time, he felt nervous
on the verge of making a business proposition. Then
Olivia started toward him with her determined, long-
legged, graceful stride and all he could think of was
what a beautiful baby they could create together.

He welcomed her with a smile.

HE'S GOING TO GIVE IT TO ME.

Olivia tingled with anticipation. Tony had been
watching her, almost studying her, all evening. And
there could only be one possible reason for that. The
sense of impending victory thrilled her.

His gaze held hers as she neared. There was that
slight tilting of his mouth—an unaffected sensual look
that she knew got all the single women and even the
not-so-single women excited. But Olivia would only
get excited if he gave her the news she wanted.

Her business was her life, and she didn't allow herself the time or the desire for anything else. She was
certain he didn't, either. At least, not with her.

She was well aware of Tony's reputation with other

women, and it was the women building that reputation. They claimed he was a spectacular lover, though how many had firsthand knowledge she couldn't guess. He appeared very circumspect to her. He never spoke of his relationships. In fact, he seemed oblivious to the talk.

She tried to be oblivious as well; her only interest in him was business related. But she had to admit there were occasions when she couldn't quite stop her mind from wandering...

She stood mere inches from him and at five-eleven or so with her heels on she nearly looked him in the eye. They stood by the balcony doors, no one else within hearing distance, the ambience soft and intimate. Olivia dismissed her wayward thoughts and lifted her glass of soda to him in a mock salute. "Tony."

"Hello, Olivia." His voice was deeper than usual, his gaze more intent. "Are you enjoying yourself?"

He seemed almost watchful, and anticipatory, not wearing the cool persona he usually assumed in her company. She looked around at the newly decorated offices, pretending an interest she didn't feel. This party was to launch the renovation of his massive downtown hotel, which had been standing for decades. With its new upscale furnishings and classy decor, it was positioned to compete with other hotels where price was no obstacle. "Everything is lovely, Tony. Why wouldn't I enjoy myself?"

His lazy smile deepened, his gaze became probing. "I don't think you're much for parties. You seem preoccupied." He tilted his head slightly. "Anxious to get back to business matters?"

Olivia swallowed her immediate response and the last sip in her glass. She allowed her gaze to follow a passing couple, then said, "I was wondering if you'd come to a decision, yet. Of course, a party isn't exactly the place to discuss such things, but..." She looked back at him and caught him watching her closely. Again. "If you'd care to enlighten me?"

Tony chuckled and ignored her question. He excelled at business games, but then, so did she. "Would you like something else to drink?"

"No, thank you," she replied.

"Had too much already?"

"Of soda? I think I can handle it. You however..." She circled his thick wrist with her fingers to bring his glass toward her and then she sniffed. But she didn't detect the fumes of alcohol. She frowned.

"I don't drink, either. Too many of my associates do, and I think someone has to stay sober to oversee things."

Olivia didn't want to show him her surprise, but she found herself doing just that. "So you never indulge?"

"An occasional glass of wine with dinner. Very occasional."

"I'm a teetotaler."

"Personal reasons?"

Olivia hesitated. It was funny how you could know a person for years and never say or do anything outside the realm of related business, then suddenly be discussing very intimate, personal topics. She didn't really mind, though. She'd always believed the better you knew your business associates the easier it would be to deal with them. It was her fondest wish to do a great many deals with Tony Austin. She finally nodded and answered, "Very personal. I detest alcohol."

"Maybe someday you'll tell me why."

"Maybe."

Tony was silent a moment. He appeared to be studying her drop-pearl earrings until suddenly he asked, "Do you have a five-year goal for yourself, Olivia? Or some long-term destination that you're working toward?"

Again, Olivia felt that touch of excitement and tried to quell it. He was showing an interest he'd never shown before, and that could only mean he approved her business management. Tony Austin was the epitome of business excellence. A person could learn everything she needed to know from him.

It was said Tony had doubled the Austin Crown hotel chain within three years of his father's death. Under Tony's guidance the hotels had grown from mediocre to posh and exclusive. Every upscale business convention around wanted to be on the receiving end of Crown's special treatment.

Tony Austin's employees loved him and praised his leadership. As a pioneer in the business world with one of the fastest growing hotel chains around, he was regularly featured in business magazines. Austin

Crown hotels were located throughout the country and probably would soon be around the world.

Olivia watched now as he propped himself up against the wall, the breadth of his shoulders visible even beneath the elegant cut of his dark suit. He was a well-built man, she admitted to herself, in his early thirties, with more energy and determination than anyone she knew. Right now his brown hair, darker and richer than her own and with a spot more curl, had fallen forward over his brow, and his green eyes were intense on her features.

Olivia smiled. "Of course I have a plan. A very substantial plan. If you'd like, I could outline it for you."

To her surprise, Tony caught one of the servers milling through the crowd. "Miss Anderson and I will be in the inner office. Please bring us refreshments, non-alcoholic only, and see that we're not bothered unless it's absolutely necessary."

The server nodded, took their empty glasses and walked away. Olivia felt her nerves tingle. *He's going to give it to me.* She hadn't expected this, hadn't expected Tony to want to discuss business tonight, but still...

Tony took her arm and began weaving through the crowd. Several people noticed, but she ignored them. Tony merely nodded to anyone who stared too long, but he was used to this. It was a fact he drew regular gossip from outsiders. After all, he was the local boy made good and there were always busybodies hoping to pick up a scrap of dirt. But they were in Willowbrook, Indiana, on Tony's home ground, and anyone who really knew him paid little heed to the rumors.

Olivia rehearsed her speech in her mind, preparing what she would say, how she would convince him to her way of thinking. She was busy wondering if she'd be able to shorten her five-year goal with his cooperation, when he tugged her into a dimly lit room that smelled of rich leather and Tony. Which, to her at least, was the scent of raw excitement. In this room she might get the break she'd been waiting for. All she had, all she would ever have, was her business. She'd given it everything she could, and it had given back all she had hoped for. Watching the business expand and grow was almost the same as having the life she really wanted. Almost.

TONY CLOSED THE DOOR and leaned against it. It was funny, but before tonight he had never really noticed how lovely Olivia Anderson could be when she was excited, when she smiled…. Of course, he'd made note of and approved each one of her individual features. But he'd never before put them all together, taken them as the whole, and understood just how tempting an appearance she made.

Tonight she had her soft dark brown hair pinned back in an elegant twist, though he knew it was nearly straight and fell to the tops of her shoulders. Olivia always looked elegant. She had more style and class than any woman he'd ever known. And it didn't matter that her eyes were dark brown, not green like his own. He liked her eyes. They showed her emotions clearly, showed the depth of her character and her passion. *Passion for her work, that is.*

He stepped away from the door and flipped on a single lamp that added a vague glow to the expansive room. It was cowardly of him, but he preferred to keep the lighting dim, to allow himself the cover of shadows while he presented her with his proposal. He said abruptly, "Have you ever been married, Olivia?"

She looked stunned by the question, but thankfully, not insulted. She shook her head. "No. Nor do I plan any such alliance in the near future."

"Alliance?" He found himself smiling again. She had the strangest way of looking at things, as if everything was a business venture.

Shrugging her shoulders, Olivia turned to find a chair, and sat down in one of a matching pair of chairs that sat adjacent to his massive desk. "My work is my life. I'm content that it stays that way."

Tony eased himself into the chair across from her, thoughtfully rubbing his chin. Though that was the answer he'd expected—anticipated—from her he was still a little disturbed. It wasn't right that a woman with her attributes, with her intelligence and personality, should spend her life alone.

"How old are you?"

She blinked, but she answered readily enough. "Twenty-six. Actually my five-year plan was only formulated last year. By the time I'm thirty, I hope to have created a very substantial business with at least three more shops."

He waved that away. "You don't leave yourself much room for a husband or children or any other personal pursuits."

Frowning now, she surveyed him with a wary eye. Tony knew he needed to retrench, to give her a bit more room. The thing was, he'd never been a patient man. When he wanted something, he wanted it now.

And he wanted a baby.

He reached out to take Olivia's hand, but she snatched it back, then looked embarrassed that she'd done so.

"I don't understand the need for such personal questions. I assumed you were satisfied with our business dealings..."

"More than satisfied. You run a very profitable business and your two existing shops have already benefited my hotels. I don't see any problem in expanding them."

Olivia let out a breath and gifted him with a beautiful smile. "Thank you. Obviously that's what I was hoping to hear. I'll admit, though, you threw me with all that personal stuff. I know it's important to understand your associates, to make certain they won't suddenly change their priorities and let their businesses flounder. If that was your worry, let me assure you—"

"I'd like to have a baby."

His timely, or not so timely, interruption, left Olivia with her mouth hanging open and her brows lifted high. It was a nice mouth, full and soft. He could see her tongue, pink and moist and... She also had beautiful skin, which of course would be a plus, along with her excellent health and unbelievable ingenuity.

She cleared her throat, and with a small, nervous laugh, said, "I believe that might be an anatomical impossibility."

"Not if I can find the right woman to carry the babe."

She fell back in her seat, her hands braced on the arms of the chair, her mouth once again open. Right then, Tony decided to stop noticing her enticing mouth.

He was saved from having to say anything by the knock on the door. Tony waited until the server left the room and softly closed the door behind him before meeting Olivia's eyes again. She still looked stunned.

"I can practically hear your brain working, Olivia, and I want to assure you, before anything else, that this has nothing to do with your business. The third shop is yours, regardless. I'll sign the papers Monday morning and have a courier deliver them to you."

Olivia's mouth opened twice before she managed to say, "Thank you."

He poured her a glass of soda and handed it to her. "However, I would like to discuss something else with you."

"I gathered as much."

He grinned at her dry tone. "As I said, I want a baby. I have excellent people who can see to the daily running of my business now, so I no longer need to put in such long hours. I can more than afford to raise a child with every privilege, but not so many that the child is spoiled or doesn't understand the value of work. I'll be very careful to make sure the babe is raised with good morals and strong convictions, and—"

Olivia leaned forward in her seat and touched his arm. Tony liked her touch, felt it all the way to his stomach, and immediately cursed himself for reacting in a way he'd forbidden. Olivia, thankfully, seemed unaware of his plight.

"I have no doubt you'd be an excellent father, Tony."

He felt warmed to his soul by her praise. "Thank you."

"You're welcome. But what does all this have to do with me?"

His gaze flickered from her hand on his arm, to her face. "Why...I want you to be the mother."

He didn't get quite the reaction he'd expected. She covered her mouth with one graceful hand, and after a long, stunned pause, a nearly hysterical laugh emerged. Tony stood, caught her forearms and lifted her from her chair. "Olivia! Are you all right?"

She shook her head, and another giggle escaped. "Didn't I just make myself clear? Didn't I just say that my business was my life? I can't get married, certainly not to—"

"Married? Good God, I don't want to marry you!" He immediately realized how horrid that sounded, and quickly explained, "I just need you to carry my baby. After you've delivered it, you're free to do as you please. I'll make certain you can relocate any place you choose, but of course, you would have to relocate. I don't want any interference with raising my child, and neither of us would want a scandal. I thought the northwest would serve your purposes."

"You just want me to..."

"Carry the baby." He was still holding her arms and felt the way she tensed, the way her body trembled. He forced himself to release her. "As you said, it's anatomically impossible for me to do so, not that I have any desire to suffer through such a thing. God in all his wisdom knew men weren't cut out for such a trial. And I don't want you to think I'm being...well, untoward. There are medical procedures that would guarantee the planting of my sperm. Everything would be..."

She staggered back as if he'd struck her.

"I'm really messing this up, aren't I?" He ran his hand through his hair, then shrugged. "Believe it or not, this is the first time I've been uncertain of myself while presenting a business proposition. And that's exactly what this is, Olivia. A business deal." He waited, but when she remained silent, her eyes huge, he added, "Well? You could make this a little easier by saying...*something*."

"I would. If I had any idea what to say."

He nodded, then slowly drew a deep breath. "You need time to think it over. Why don't we sit back down and I'll go over all my reasons for choosing you, all the benefits that will be yours if you agree, how I intend to handle the legalities involved, and—"

"That's an awful lot of ground to cover, especially considering it's near midnight. I put in a full day already, and plan to visit the office tomorrow morning." Her voice still sounded shaky, but she did resume her seat. Tony let out a short sigh of relief. She wasn't crying sexual harassment, she wasn't storming out. No, Olivia, bless her, was a reasonable woman. It was one of the qualities that had drawn him to her.

"First of all, you please me very much, Olivia. Not as a wife or for any other personal relationship, but as a gene donor. Your intelligence sometimes staggers me, especially given what few advantages you had in the world. The way you've excelled—"

"Excuse me?"

Tony lifted his brows, silently asking for clarification to her interruption.

"How, exactly, would you know anything about my advantages or disadvantages?"

Uh-oh. He could tell by the mulish set to her chin that he'd pricked her temper. He quickly thought about lying, then just as quickly discarded the idea. As he'd said, she was very intelligent. "I had you investigated. Now, just hear me out, then you'll understand how necessary it was for me to do so." He waited, and when she simply watched him, he began reciting his findings. "I know your parents, of moderate, low middle-class income, died in a river accident during a flood when you were only sixteen. I know you carried a full course load in college and kept a job at the same time, that you gained everything you now own by your own wits, without a single smidgen of aid from family or friends. In fact, there was no real family, and as far as I could discern, no close friends."

He continued, seeing her hold herself silent and still. She managed to look both proud and violated, and he lowered his tone even more, feeling his heart kick against his ribs. "You've never been involved with a man for any length of time other than during business to further your goals, you live a modest, understated life-style, apparently with quite a substantial savings account, and you keep to yourself. The only social gatherings you attend are business related."

She was quiet a long moment, and he felt regret, then determination.

"You've been very thorough."

"I had to make certain you would suit, Olivia. Please, try to understand. I don't want a woman who, after conceiving, will decide she wants to keep the baby, me, or both. Everything I learned about you proves you have absolutely no interest in tying yourself down right now or anytime in the near future. It was completely necessary that I find evidence to prove you wouldn't want a baby or a husband. And you don't, do you?"

She turned her head away to stare at the far wall. "That's right." After a shuddering breath, she glared at him again. "But I also have no interest in putting myself nine months behind. Carrying a child right now would sorely interrupt my schedule, not to mention what it would do to my reputation. I'd be gossiped about endlessly."

"Not so. Not if I promised to advance your five-year goal in one year. Not if I promised my backing to make certain you got a better start than you could ever have hoped to achieve, even in five years. Not if I have you relocated immediately, or provide for you to take an extended leave of absence."

"And you'd do all that?"

She was incredulous, but he didn't hesitate. "Of course. I'm very serious about this. I can afford to be generous, and I want the baby. Now. My birthday is November 14. Little more than a week away. By my following birthday, I want to be holding my own child. I'll be thirty-five then." He hesitated, a bit vulnerable in his feelings, but also knowing he needed to explain his desire fully to her.

"Thirty-five is getting up there. If I'm going to have a baby, it needs to be now. I'm still young enough to keep up with a toddler, but old enough to make wise decisions about the child's future. If I wait, even another year or two, I'll be close to forty before the child is born. I have to think long-term, of how my age will affect the child during his or her teenage years, when I'll be needed most."

She looked incredulous again, and her voice was strained when she asked, "You're worried about your...your biological clock?"

He felt disgruntled with the way she'd put it, but he nodded. "I suppose that's one way of looking at it."

"Why?"

"Why what?"

"Why do you want a child so badly? Why not just get a wife and do things the conventional way? And most of all, why me?"

Since she was still discussing it with him, Tony decided that was a good sign and took heart. He would win her over. After all, he had the advantage, being a man, and a more accomplished business dealer. He'd wrangled tougher deals than this when he'd first taken over the business.

But also true, he'd met few associates as tough as Olivia. It was one of the reasons he'd chosen her, one of the many things he admired about her.

He propped his elbows on his knees, leaned forward and forged on. "I want a child now because both my younger brother and sister have children. In fact, my brother only recently got his third child, a little boy, and it made me realize how much I was missing out on, how much I'll miss forever if I don't act soon. Don't get me wrong. I love being the doting uncle, getting to spoil the children and having them shout and jump around whenever I show up. It's good for the soul to be loved by a child, probably the biggest compliment a person can ever receive.

"But I have no real influence on the kids. And that's as it should be. I'm not their father, I'm only an uncle, good for bringing gifts and giving occasional unimportant advice. I want to be the one doing the raising, leaving a part of myself behind.''

Olivia smiled. ''You're feeling your mortality?''

''I suppose. But that's not all of it. Being business minded, forming a successful company and being respected by your colleagues, that's nothing compared to raising a child. My brother and sister chose not to get too involved in the business, but they're raising wonderful, loving, beautiful children. And that's a much greater accomplishment than mine. I want to do something that matters that much.'' He faced her, holding her gaze, then added, ''And I want to be loved the way they are. Unconditionally, completely.''

''But no wife?''

''The kind of relationship my brother and sister have with their spouses doesn't come easy, I'm finding.'' He was so relieved she hadn't mocked him that he smiled. It was proving much easier to talk to Olivia than he had thought. Without thinking about it, he'd bared his heart as he had never done with any other person. ''It's almost like they're one with the other. They share everything, support each other, and they have fun together. Honest, guilt-free fun. They seem to know each others' thoughts sometimes, they're so in tune.

''It amazes me. At times, I'm even jealous. I think it would be unbelievable to have that kind of relationship, and after seeing it, I don't think I could settle for anything less. But I haven't found a woman who would suit, and to tell you the truth, I'm sick of looking. Most women can't tolerate the amount of time I dedicate to the business, unless they're business-women also. But then, most of them are so wrapped up in company policies, in proving themselves in the male-dominant corporate world, they don't have time for me, much less a child."

He saw her flinch, and realized she'd taken the criticism personally. "Olivia. I don't mean to condemn. I realize it's more difficult for women than men, that the same rules seldom apply. And I understand the need to get ahead. I was the same way until recently."

"Until your business no longer required quite so much attention."

"That's right." He wouldn't apologize for accomplishing his goals. He'd earned his time off. "You know, there's a downside to being successful. I always get the feeling women are sizing up my bank account instead of me."

Olivia gawked. "Don't you have any idea how attractive you are? How personable you are?" She waved a hand in the air. "How...*sensual* you are? Believe me, with or without your hotel chain, you'd have women chasing after you."

Settling back in his chair, he whispered, "Not you."

Olivia looked as if she wanted to bite off her tongue, but no way would Tony let her take the words back, nor would he fill the silence for her. He suddenly felt predatory, and she was his prey. He could feel the surge of energy her words had given him, supplying an interest he hadn't felt in too long. It was invigorating, though he did his best to ignore the feelings and concentrate on his goals. Her compliments weren't necessary to his plan—but they did fill him with male satisfaction.

He waited, his expectation extreme, to see what she would say next.

Her gaze never wavered. "Well, no. As I said, I have other goals in mind besides chasing down a man, regardless of his appeal."

Tony narrowed his eyes, watching her squirm as he pondered her words, then he smiled. "That's one of the reasons I chose you. Not once have you ever looked at me in a sexual way."

Olivia blinked again. "I don't think..."

"You know what I mean. I don't have to worry about you accepting my proposition with ulterior motives of trapping me, because you don't particularly want me." He waited, then asked, "Right?"

"Ah...right."

"But you are perfect to suit me. As I said, I admire your intelligence. With the two of us as parents, I know my son or daughter won't be lacking in that regard. You're also possessed of a great deal of savvy, something else to admire. You're healthy as a horse. I checked back as far as the last two years, and you haven't missed a single day of work. You have a kind and generous nature—everyone who knows you said so. And you're suitably built."

"Suitably built?"

She sounded as though she were strangling, and his gaze dropped to her legs. "Attractively built," he explained, allowing his gaze to linger for a moment. "Your legs are shapely, your shoulders squared, your back straight. You're large boned, not overly frail, but still very feminine. You're not prone to excess weight, but you are...sturdy. If I had a daughter, I wouldn't have to worry about her being too tiny, something I abhor in women. But she would make a very nice appearance. You always do."

Without his mind's permission, his gaze moved to her breasts, outlined so nicely by the black knit dress she wore. Tony heard her say, "I'm small busted."

He managed a shrug when at the moment he felt far from indifferent, then had to force himself to look up at her face. Her look was challenging, and he grinned at her small show of vanity. "Not at all. You're...fine. Besides, if I have a son, it certainly won't matter, and if I have a daughter, I won't have to worry about all the young men chasing after her before I'm prepared to deal with it."

She gave an uncertain smile at his wit, then looked away, as if considering all he'd said. He felt his stomach cramping in anxiety. And something more. It was so damn ridiculous, but the more he talked with her, the more he liked her. She hadn't reacted as most women would have, she hadn't reeled in shock or shouted in dismay. She hadn't looked particularly insulted, either. She did look a bit disoriented, though. And somewhat contemplative.

He didn't want to, but he said, "Why don't you think about it? Take the weekend, and get back to me on

Monday. If you agree, we can contact the doctor I've spoken with and have everything taken care of well before my birthday."

She winced. "A clinical procedure, you said?"

"Yes." He hastened to reassure her. "But from what I understand, it's not bad. I deliver my sperm—"

One slim eyebrow quirked. "Deliver your sperm?"

"Yes." He knew his face was heating and felt like a fool.

"How exactly is that accomplished?"

"Never mind." The order was ground out from between his teeth, and she chuckled. He'd never before seen her sense of humor; usually it was her determination to get ahead that she presented at a business meeting. He felt a touch of warmth at the sound of her laughter, then gave her an exasperated look and continued. "I deliver my sperm and they...well, I suppose it's much like visiting your gynecologist. Only instead of doing whatever it is they usually do, my sperm will be artificially planted—inseminated, it's called—and then we'll wait to see if it takes."

Olivia chewed her lips, then said slowly, "It sounds rather distasteful."

"I'll admit it isn't quite the way nature intended a woman to be impregnated, but it is certainly less personal, which is the main objective."

"Why?"

Her pointed look and bald question confused him. "Why what?"

"Why does it have to be so impersonal? Why can't you just...do it?"

"Do it?"

She made a sound of disgust. "Just impregnate the woman of your choice by nature's design."

He knew what she was asking, and felt an instant, unwanted tightening in his loins. Lust, damnable lust. He swallowed. "I want this to be as much of a business dealing as possible. Getting naked..." He felt himself harden and had to clear his throat. "Making love to a woman isn't at all a business proposition. It's very personal."

Olivia seemed relaxed now, arrogantly so, and somehow determined. Tony knew she was aware of his unease, and planned to take advantage of it—as any good businesswoman would do. She nodded, a pseudo show of understanding. Then she smiled. "I see."

He felt a twinge of anger at her for prodding him. "I should hope so."

"I believe I'll take your advice and think all this over. You said you don't want to hear from me until Monday?"

"I..." He had no idea what had come over her. She wasn't acting the way he'd expected, she wasn't even acting in a way he could have guessed or anticipated. He felt stymied. "You don't have to wait if you come to a decision before then."

"I think I probably will make up my mind before

then. How about if I give you my decision tomorrow evening?"

He nodded, stiff-backed now, and forced a smile. He knew by her amused expression that she wasn't fooled, and that she was thoroughly enjoying his discomfort. "I'll give you my home number."

"No. I got the feeling you didn't want the fertile woman who would serve your needs to intrude on your life." He started to speak, but she forestalled him, her tone not nearly so sarcastic now. "Why don't I just give you my number instead—my privacy isn't nearly as threatened as your own. You can call me. Say, seven o'clock tomorrow?"

With her small chin raised, her straight nose in the air, she looked as proud and gutsy and almost as arrogant as he. She looked magnificent to him, and he merely nodded, distracted by thoughts of her feminine body rounded by his babe. They would make a beautiful, healthy child together. He reached out and touched her chin. "I wouldn't mind if the baby was a boy or a girl. I don't remember if I told you that."

She smiled, and seemed to relax again despite herself. "You didn't. But I had the impression it wouldn't matter." Then she went to his desk and picked up the gold pen from the marble holder and scrawled her home number across the desk pad."

"I had your number in my files."

"This way, you won't have to look it up."

He felt awkward now, but Olivia didn't seem to be

suffering any such problems. She gave him a small salute.

"I'll be going home now. It's getting late, and I do have quite a bit to think over."

"I'll be a good father, Olivia." He hadn't meant to say that. He hadn't planned on trying to convince her what a good person he was. But he wanted the baby so badly, now, before he got any older, before he was left all alone in the world.

Again, she didn't mock him.

"I never doubted it." She looked almost sad, which didn't make any sense. "Tomorrow at seven, Tony." And then she was gone.

2

OLIVIA LAY IN BED that night, despising herself. She was a fraud and a manipulator and the worst kind of person for taking advantage of another. Tony had no idea the type of woman he was dealing with.

She'd known since she was sixteen that she would never have children. For her, it was physically impossible.

In the hospital, only hours before Olivia's mother had slipped away, she had explained about the condition that robbed her daughter of that particular function. Olivia wasn't a whole woman, could never lead a whole life. Having children was as beyond her as it was for Tony. And so she'd made her business her life. It was the only life she'd ever have.

Swallowing hard, Olivia felt the sting of tears as she recalled going to the hospital as a very young girl, her belly cramping painfully, the bleeding. It had been horrible, being examined by a male doctor. Beyond the pain, she'd felt violated and mortified. And then there were the days after when her mother and father had been so quiet, so withdrawn. She hated hospitals now, and she wouldn't go to the doctor unless it was absolutely necessary.

She thought she'd successfully put the past behind her, that she'd buried the wishes that couldn't come true. But now, with Tony's proposition, they all came flooding back. She wanted to be loved, to have children, to be desired by a special man who would accept her as a sensual woman.

She couldn't do anything about the first two wishes, but the third was a possibility.

It was rumored that Tony was an exceptional lover. She couldn't deny that the information had given her a few private fantasies of her own. After all, despite everything, she was still a woman, and on occasion, she'd seen him strictly as a man. But intimacy was something she'd neither expected nor wanted from Tony.

Until she'd heard his plan.

And now it was all she could think about. Tony obviously admired her, and that was something. It wasn't love, but it was a far cry from a totally detached sexual experience. She cared about Tony, thought he was a beautiful person and a very sexy man. And he wanted her as the mother of his child.

That was a precious gift all on its own, the highest of compliments.

Tony didn't have to know that she'd never be able to conceive a child, that she was infertile. She could insist on doing things the "natural" way, allow him to try his manly best for a couple of weeks, then confess it wasn't happening. He'd go on his way, none the wiser, find another woman, and have his baby by his designated time. She had not a single doubt of his eventual success. There were numerous women out there who would be more than willing to oblige him.

But he'd approached her, and she couldn't quite send him on his way. Not yet. Hearing him discuss his sperm in such a casual way, and talk of impregnating her as if he was referring to buying her coffee, had been somehow very arousing. Long dormant feelings had seemed to swell without her consent, and when she'd pictured him "supplying" his sperm, pictured the process necessary to such a deed, she'd felt a sexual heat at the image, along with an emotional tenderness that he wanted a child so badly. Together, the two feelings had conspired against her better sense.

She'd read every article she could ever find on him, and they were numerous. She'd tried to follow in his footsteps, as impossible as that seemed, because he was too dynamic, too overwhelming. And also, he loved his family, when she didn't even have a family to claim.

He was a good man, in every sense of the word. And she planned to corrupt him for her own purposes.

She was a fraud, but she wouldn't actually be hurting anyone. Other than herself.

IT HAD PROVED to be a long night and an even longer day. By seven o'clock, Olivia was so nervous her heart threatened to beat right out of her chest. When her phone rang, a good three minutes after seven, she jumped a foot. She forced herself to wait through four rings, feeling juvenile but determined not to look over-anxious, and then she answered.

"Hello?"

"Olivia? It's Tony."

Just that, nothing more. She cleared her throat. "Hello." Her voice squeaked, but she didn't hang up. She could do this; she would grab the opportunity. But of course, she wouldn't accept anything from him, other than the additional shop he'd already agreed to. She would suffer no guilt for taking monetary advantage of him. She would only use his body, and only for a brief time.

"Hi." There was a long pause. "Have you made up your mind?"

She bit her lips, then took a deep breath. "I have. But I...I have a few stipulations I'd like to discuss."

She heard his indrawn breath. "Does that mean you'll do it?"

"Yes. But with a few—"

"I heard you. A few stipulations. Whatever it is, it's yours!"

His joy was impossible to ignore. The man was thrilled to be getting what he believed would eventually be his baby. Olivia swallowed her guilt and girded herself. "You probably ought to know what I want before you agree to it."

"I can afford whatever it is. I know you're not a greedy woman. You won't leave me bankrupt."

"I want to forget the doctor."

Deathly quiet. "Excuse me?"

Olivia knew she had thrown that out there awfully quick, but if she hadn't, she might never have said it at all. "I don't want to go through a doctor. I want...I want to do things naturally."

"Naturally?"

He sounded completely stupefied, and she nearly growled in frustration. "Yes, dammit! As in you and me, together, the way nature intended."

Not a single sound now. "Tony?"

"I'm here."

Olivia waited. Strangely enough, she could hear Tony trying to sort his thoughts as clearly as she could hear her own heart pounding.

Finally he said, "Would you mind telling me why?"

Olivia shook her head, realized how stupid that was and closed her eyes. "Of course not. I just..."

"No, wait. This isn't a conversation for the phone. Are you busy?"

"Now?"

"Yes, now. Believe me, I don't want to have to sleep on this without understanding."

"Of course not." Olivia looked around her apartment, hoping for inspiration, but found only the same quiet environment that always surrounded her. "I could meet you somewhere."

"No, I'll pick you up. I know where you live. It's—"

"It's in your records."

"Yes. I'll be there as soon as I can."

The phone clicked in her ear, and to Olivia it sounded like the beginning of a drumroll. Oh boy, too late to change her mind now. Then, because she had no idea how far away Tony was or how soon he would arrive, she rushed from the room to find something appropriate to wear.

When she reached her closet, she stopped, feeling ridiculous. What in the world would be considered proper dress for telling a man you'd agree to have his baby, but only if he'd pleasure you in the bargain?

Especially when you knew you were cheating him, and he wouldn't get a damn thing out of the deal, least of all, what he really wanted. A baby.

TONY STARED at her apartment door, started to knock, then lowered his hand. Dammit all, why couldn't women ever do anything the simple way? He'd offered Olivia a straightforward, up-front deal, and she'd had to go and muddy the waters by asking that he actually attend her. Not that it would be a hardship, but he didn't want to get involved. He'd made his plans and he didn't want to deviate from them.

Still, Olivia Anderson—business barracuda and proprietor of two sensual, sexy lingerie shops—wanted to make love with him.

Who would have ever thought she'd ask for such a thing? She was always an enigma, a mix of styles and personalities, but even so, this development had thrown him for a loop. He'd sometimes wondered, when he'd been in her shop and seen the very stimulating garments she carried, if *she* ever wore any of those little bits of nothing, if she spoiled her body with silks and lace. It hadn't seemed likely. But now...

She had him totally confused, and he didn't like it one bit. He also didn't want to have to start looking for a new mother. Time was running out. He wasn't getting any younger, and if he didn't act soon, he'd be past the age of thirty-five when he brought his baby home.

No. He'd chosen her, dammit, and he wouldn't give up without at least trying to reason with her.

He ran a hand through his hair, then knocked sharply on the door. Immediately three doors opened. Olivia and two neighbors stared at him, the latter with narrowed eyes and curious expressions. Just what he needed, an engrossed audience.

Olivia tried for a smile, but it wasn't her best effort. "Come on inside."

"No." He shook his head, glaring at the neighbors. An elderly couple now stood at one door, and a younger woman with curlers in her hair at the other; they glared right back at him. Tony turned his gaze back to Olivia. "Let's go for a drive instead."

Olivia hesitated, seemingly oblivious to the onlookers, then finally said, "All right. Just let me grab my jacket."

Tony cursed under his breath. This was exactly what he'd wanted to avoid. He didn't need anyone speculating on his relationship with Olivia, because he'd never intended to have a relationship with her. In his simple, uncomplicated, male-inspired plan, he would have given her the address of the doctor and then heard from her later to learn if she'd conceived. He certainly hadn't intended to stand in her doorway providing entertainment to the masses. Not that three people could be considered a mass, but with their eyes glued to him, he felt very uncomfortable.

Olivia finally produced herself. She stepped outside the door, turned to make certain it was locked, then dropped her keys into her pocket. "I'm ready."

Then, as if on cue, she turned to the neighbors and nodded to each one in turn. "Hello, Hilda, Leroy, Emma. This is Tony Austin. Hopefully I'll be opening another of my shops in his hotel chain. Isn't that marvelous?"

Everyone nodded, their suspicions visibly dissipating and en masse they began to sing Olivia's praises. Tony did his best to make an exit, but he had to spend several minutes nodding in agreement before he could leave.

As they walked out of the building onto the street, he said, "That's the last time for that."

"What?"

"Meeting at your apartment. It gives rise to too much speculation. If we're not careful, we'll have that scandal yet."

He opened the door to his car for Olivia, but she didn't get in. "Does that mean you intend to meet with me again? You will agree with my terms?"

Pushy woman. Why had he never realized before just how pushy she could be? Savvy was one thing, pushy was another. He summoned his most noncommittal tone. "We'll see." He practically tossed her into the passenger seat, before going around to his own side.

"There's really not a whole lot to see, Tony. I don't like the idea of the clinical approach, that's all. If you can't see your way clear to actually touch me, then there's nothing to talk about."

He clenched his hands on the steering wheel. He clenched his teeth. He even clenched his thighs, but still, her words affected him. Touch her? He'd like to touch her all right—now, this very minute, with his hands, his mouth, his entire body. But he wouldn't. Oh, no. Touching was bad. Touching would only lead to more touching, and then he'd be in over his head and...

"Tony?"

"How about doing me a favor, Olivia? How about keeping your thoughts to yourself for a few minutes until we get off the road and then we'll discuss your...terms."

"All right."

She sounded too damn agreeable and that rankled, but at least she kept her words behind her teeth for all of five minutes, giving him a blessed chance to gain control of his libido. Then she asked in a very tentative voice, "Have you considered the possibility that I won't conceive? After all, there's no guarantee that I'll prove to be...fertile ground for you to...plant your seed. How much time are you willing to devote to trying to get me pregnant?"

Fertile ground? Plant his seed? Tony's five minutes of calm were suddenly shot to hell. How was it such bland, ridiculous terms sounded sexier than the most erotic whispered words he'd ever heard? Perhaps it was because of the envisioned result. He'd never before considered a woman carrying his child, and that must be the reason every word out of her mouth aroused him to the point of pain.

He cleared his throat and kept his gaze steady on the darkened road. "The doctor mentioned that several attempts may be necessary before the insemination takes."

"But doing it naturally? Is there a projected time span on that?"

He felt strangled. "I never actually asked him that."

"Perhaps you should."

Out of sheer necessity, he pulled the car off the main street and onto a small dirt road that led to a dead end. When Tony was younger, he and his brother had come here to make out with girls. In those days there was a wide cornfield, but it had been replaced by a small park with a street lamp. Obviously things had changed, but the premise was the same. Isolation.

Despite the fact that he was sweating, he left the car running, for it was a cold night in early November. He killed the lights, though, giving himself some illusionary concealment. When he turned to face her, he already had his mouth open to start his argument, but he was brought up short by the picture she presented.

Moonlight poured over her, revealing the sheen of

dark hair, the shape of her ears, her high arched brows. Her eyelashes left long feathery shadows on her cheeks and shielded her eyes from his gaze. Her hands were folded in her lap. She appeared somehow very unsure of herself...vulnerable. It wasn't a look he was used to, not from her. She lifted her gaze to his face, and once again he felt that deep frustration.

It wasn't that Olivia was beautiful. She was by far the most elegant woman he'd ever known, but she wasn't classically beautiful. He had dated more attractive women, made love to them, had long-standing affairs with them that had left him numb. But Olivia was the only woman whose personality, intelligence and disposition were attractive enough to entice him into asking her to carry his child. That was something. More than something, actually, when you figured it was usually looks that drew a man first, and the other, more important features of a woman that kept him drawn.

When he remained quiet, she said, "I know what I'm asking seems absurd. After all, you could have any woman you want, and after knowing you for so long, it's obvious you don't particularly want me. That's okay, because up until you mentioned your plan, I hadn't really thought about wanting you, either.

"But you see, I've made my career everything." Her hands twisted in her lap and her voice shook. "Just as you don't want any involvements now, neither do I. That's why the idea seems so perfect. I haven't taken the time or the effort to get to know very many men, and almost never on an intimate level. These days, only an idiot would indulge in casual sex. But starting a relationship isn't something I want, either. So I thought, maybe we could both get what we wanted."

Tony searched her face, feeling dumbfounded. Surely she wasn't suggesting what he thought she was. "I want a baby. What is it you want, Olivia?"

She turned her head away from him and looked out the window. Sounding so unlike herself, she whispered in a small voice, "I want a wild, hot, never-to-be-forgotten affair. For two weeks. If during that time I conceive, the baby will become yours, and we'll go on with the rest of your plans. If I don't conceive, I'll be on my way and you can find another woman who, hopefully, will prove more fertile. You won't owe me a thing. In fact, I'll consider myself well paid."

"*Well paid?* As in sex? You make yourself sound like a..."

"Like a woman who's desperate? I suppose I am." She finally met his gaze, her eyes huge and so very dark in the dim light. "I want to know what it's like to be with a man. But it has to be a man I trust, both with my safety and my health. I'm afraid you fit that bill."

The way she'd worded that had him frowning. "Olivia, you're not a virgin, are you?"

"No, but close." She held up two slim fingers.

"You've had sex with two different men?"

"No, I've had sex twice. With the same man, or boy rather. Neither time necessarily inspired an encore, but the second time I allowed myself to be convinced. I suppose I was hoping he'd improved from the week before, but he hadn't."

Tony found himself smiling. Olivia wanted to have sex with him, but she planned to keep a score card? "What did he do that was so wrong?"

"I'm not certain I know what was wrong, since I haven't yet experienced it *right*, but we were both practically fully clothed, cramped into the back seat of his car, and he grunted a lot. And by a lot, I mean for all of about three minutes. Continuously."

"Well..." Tony suppressed a laugh and tried to look serious. "I suppose I can improve on that, anyway."

"I should certainly hope so."

Tony couldn't help but chuckle at her serious tone. "I can't recall ever having a woman come right out and ask me to perform to her satisfaction. You're downright scary, do you know that?"

"I don't mean to be. And I don't mean to belittle that guy. We were in college, and he was majoring in football. It was probably my fault for not being more discriminating my first and second time, but even then I was very involved in getting ahead. Choosing an ideal mate simply took more energy than I wanted to give. At the time, it hadn't occurred to me to tell him specifically what I did and didn't like, which probably would have made things better. But now, since you've presented yourself on the proverbial silver platter, I can hope the results will be much more to my liking. After all, you have a reputation for fulfilling such expectations."

Reputation? He didn't even want to get into that with her. If she'd been listening to gossip... Well, at least the gossip appeared to have been flattering. He gave a groan that was loud and rife with confusion. "I just don't know, Olivia. I mean, this could all backfire."

She was all business, not moved in the least by his dramatic display of frustration. "You're afraid I'll be privy to your awesome technique, decide I can't possibly live without it or you and want to stake a marital claim?"

Actually she was pretty close to the mark. Not that he believed his technique was really all that awesome. But he knew women too often associated sex with love. He'd have to make it clear to her...

"I understand how you feel, Tony. I was concerned also, only for opposite reasons. Right now, you only want a baby, but as you see the woman who will give you your child grow, as you see the changes in her body—from you and your baby—are you certain you won't transfer your affection for the child to the mother?"

He stared stupidly. "I hadn't planned to watch any changes."

"No? But I understood, from books I read long ago, that the changes were the most fascinating part. You won't want to feel your baby kick? You won't want to be in on any prenatal pictures taken? I saw a documentary on TV once that was incredible. The ultrasound showed every small movement the baby made. You could even count toes and fingers."

His head began to pound with the growing complications. "I think...I think I may have more to think about."

"I'm sorry. Now I've confused you."

"You haven't confused me. It's just that I hadn't even considered prenatal observation. All my thoughts had been directed solely on the baby after its birth. But of course I'd want to see and feel the changes." He studied her closely. "You wouldn't mind?"

"Mind what?"

"If I watched you closely? If I observed all the changes in your body while my baby grew and if I examined those changes, took part in them?"

She was silent again, her fingers worrying the edge of her coat. Then she shook her head and in a hushed tone, she replied, "No. I wouldn't mind. If that was what you wanted—and if I got pregnant."

"Olivia, there's no reason to doubt you will. You're a healthy young woman, in the prime of your childbearing years. I've already been checked, and the doctor assures me I should possess sufficient potency to see the job done."

Olivia drew a deep breath and then held out her hand. "So. Do we have a deal?"

He was so aroused, he knew his hand would shake like the skinny branches on the naked tree shadowing the park, but he took her small palm in his anyway. His voice was little more than a croak when he said, "A deal."

"When do we start?"

She may as well have said, *when do you want to see me naked and touch me and come inside me,* because the effect was the same. He had trouble drawing a breath as images too erotic to bear shot through his already muddled brain. It took all his masculine power to bring himself back in order. "I suppose you should find out when you're..." He gulped, then forged manfully onward. "When you're most fertile. Do you, ah, keep track of such things?"

"Of course. All women do, if they don't want to be taken by surprise. How about if I let you know, then we'll see what works for both of us?"

It irritated him no end that she could speak so calmly after practically ordering him to pleasure her, to make certain he loved her in a way she would never forget. His brain was busy concentrating on the myriad ways he'd see the job done; he could barely form coherent words, damn her. "That's fine."

"I'll look at my calendar, find out exactly when I'm most likely to conceive, and then I'll call you."

"And you will take my home number now, Olivia. I don't want to miss your call if I'm not in the office when...when you're ready."

Her smile now was confident and made his insides twist. "Whatever you say, Tony."

Tony merely gulped, wondering if she would say that when she was naked beneath him, her thighs open, her womb ready to receive him and his sperm, her body his. He kept silent, words well beyond him, and determined to see the job done as quickly as possible. It was the only way to save his sanity.

OLIVIA SPENT THE REST of the weekend boning up on fertility procedures. Though she didn't really have a regular cycle that could be timed and knew there was no chance she'd get pregnant, she thought it would still be easier to do things in the proper course, just so Tony wouldn't get suspicious. She had to be able to claim a day her period would be due, so Tony wouldn't think they'd been precipitous in their efforts.

When she decided to claim her best time would be that weekend, she suffered through a mixture of anticipation, guilt and plain old self-doubt. But she shook off her insecurities. Monday, after the new contract arrived, just as Tony had said it would, she used it as an excuse to get in touch with him.

She rushed the contract past her lawyer, insisting he give it top priority. If he thought her request unusual, he didn't say so. He returned it, with a few minor changes, the next day. Olivia forced herself to take another day to look it over, but she okay'd it without her usual relentless perusal, then picked up the phone to set up a business luncheon through Tony's secretary. It was only Wednesday morning, four days after she'd gotten Tony's agreement, and already it felt like forever since the deal had been made.

Just as she hoped, his secretary came back with the news that Tony could make time to see her at their usual restaurant. They'd met there before to discuss business, but today was different. Olivia left her office with the contract in her briefcase, along with a book on fertility and an anticipatory smile on her face.

TONY WAS ALREADY SEATED when she arrived. He'd chosen an isolated table at the back of the restaurant, away from prying eyes and ears. Olivia silently approved his choice, and forced herself to greet him in a normal, businesslike manner. Tony stood until she was seated, his eyes never leaving her, then waited while the waitress handed them menus. Very few things, including excitement, ever dampened her appetite so she ordered a lunch of rich soup and a salad.

Tony surveyed her a moment longer, then asked, "You have a problem with the agreement I sent you?"

Olivia waved away his concern. "We only made a few minor alterations."

"You always have alterations, Olivia, but I'd rarely call them minor."

She grinned. He was right, after all. She was a shark, but proud of it. "You can't expect me to blindly accept rules of your making, now can you, Tony? The revised contract will suit my purpose much better, as you'll see."

He gave her a small smile. "I don't doubt I'll approve it. I seldom win with you."

The way he said that, with a touch of pride, confused her. Could he have been telling the complete truth, not just trying to gain her acceptance of his plan? Did he truly admire her business skills? She felt warmed by the very idea, especially since most of her other male associates either seemed intimidated by her or resentful of her confidence.

She sent Tony a cheeky grin and said, "You win all too often, anyway. Losing on occasion is good for your character."

"But winning's more fun." Then he held up a hand. "In this case, though, you didn't have to bother your lawyer. I already told you I'd give you whatever you wanted."

"No."

"Beg your pardon?"

Olivia wanted to make her point perfectly clear. Her conscience was nagging her enough about manipulating him emotionally. She certainly couldn't do so professionally, too. "I want this latest agreement to stand on its own, Tony. It doesn't have anything to do with...the other. Look over the agreement, judge it the same way you would any other, then get back to me."

"And you'll relent if I don't approve of your changes?"

"Absolutely not." She gave him another grin. "But I fully expect to have to work for them if they're not to your liking."

He looked amused, his chin propped in his palm, his elbow on the table. Then his gaze dropped to his napkin and he said, "Do you have anything else to discuss with me, Olivia?"

It was more than obvious what he was asking. She set down her salad fork and then pushed her plate to the side. After hefting her briefcase into her lap, she pulled out a slim volume on fertility and flipped the book open to the page she had marked.

Tony merely stared, his slouched position not so slouched now.

"I've been reading up on our latest subject, and it seems this weekend will be my most promising time. According to this book, I should be ovulating on Saturday, give or take a day."

"So you're due in two weeks? Right at the end of the deadline you set?"

Her two week time limit. Get her pregnant by then, or the deal was off. She almost groaned at her own audacity.

"That's right. Two weeks exactly." Actually she'd pulled that ridiculous number out of the air, just as she'd done with the deadline. She wouldn't conceive, not with only one ovary. And her periods were irregular, often nonexistent, so there was no true time frame. You couldn't get pregnant if you didn't ovulate, which was a fact she'd been living with for a very long time.

It was pure coincidence that she'd set up her most fertile time to fall precisely within her deadline. She glanced up and wished she wore reading glasses, just to provide her with a bit of camouflage. But despite her embarrassment, she was determined to follow through. Tony had been more than a little reluctant to agree to her terms, and if this was to be her one big romantic rendezvous, she wanted his wholehearted involvement. She *needed* his wholehearted involvement. As with any deal, success required planning. And Olivia had formulated her plan well. By the time she was finished with him, Tony would be beyond ready; he'd be anxious.

She braced herself and said, "I think I can get a few days away. How about you?"

"A few days?"

"Well of course." Olivia frowned at him. "According to the book, an extended amount of time might be necessary. Listen to this. *The couple should have intercourse at least twice with an interval of six hours between.* You see? There's no reason to do it if we aren't going to do it with proper enthusiasm. Things like this can't be rushed."

"I, ah..."

"There's something else, too."

Tony raised his brows, not deigning and frankly not able to verbalize at this point.

Olivia forged on. "It also mentions you should do without sex until then to allow your sperm count to build to a higher level." She paused, taking a small sip of her tea, then pinning him with her gaze. She felt horribly deceptive, but determined just the same. This was to be *her* time, and hers alone. "You should be celibate until we're together. Will that be a problem?"

"Olivia..."

She hurried to explain, wanting him to understand the supposed reasoning behind her request. It wouldn't do for him to know her remarks were

prompted by a possessive attitude, rather than a legit-
imate concern. "You don't want to deplete your sperm,
Tony, now do you?"

"No."

"Good." Olivia didn't want to admit to the relief she
felt, and she certainly didn't want Tony to witness it, so
she busied herself by smoothing back another page.
Tony looked down and his eyes narrowed at the number of lines she'd highlighted. Olivia quickly tried to
close the book, but Tony's finger got in the way.

"What's this? Other interesting facts you've made
note of?" His voice sounded deeper than usual, and a
little hoarse.

Olivia was very careful not to look at him. "A few."

"They apply to us?" When she only nodded, he said,
"Please, enlighten me."

"Perhaps it would be better to wait until later—"

"But I'm dying of curiosity."

His mocking tone brought her head up. "All right."
She held the book before her and made a show of clearing her throat. She'd bluffed her way through more
than one difficult situation without losing her poise. "It
also says, *For further assurance of success the woman
should lie still on her back for several minutes, preferably
with the man still inside her, with her legs bent at the knee to
allow a pool of sperm to remain near the cervix.*"

Tony had just taken a sip from his glass as Olivia began her discourse. When he choked, spewing water
across the small table, Olivia leaned over and pounded
on his back, nearly unseating him. He caught her hand

and stared at her, his face turning ruddy, until she finally subsided and pulled away.

Olivia felt satisfied with his reaction. If she could keep him off guard, he wouldn't stand a chance of dissecting her motivation and discovering her perfidy. "Surely you know all this already? It was your idea after all."

"No." He vehemently shook his head. "My idea did not include *staying still inside you for several minutes.*"

"You find the idea repellent?" She did her best to look affronted, knowing his problem now didn't stem from distaste, but rather from the intimate level of the conversation—and possibly his response to it. "You would prefer, of course, that I lie on a sterile table while a damn white-coated doctor probed me with a syringe?"

"Olivia..." He reached across the table and took her hand again. "I don't think you have any idea how all of this is affecting me. I'm only a man, you know, and I'm not accustomed to this sort of conversation."

His hand felt warm and dry and very large. Olivia closed her eyes, then experienced another wave of guilt. She was twitting him mercilessly for her own benefit, and he was having difficulty surviving it. "I'm sorry. I shouldn't carry on. The truth is," she added, hoping just a touch of honesty would help smooth over the situation, "I'm a little uncomfortable, too. I'm trying to be as straightforward and open about this as I can, so that we can look at it in a purely businesslike fashion."

"I know, and I understand." He hesitated, then released her fingers and leaned back in his chair. His gaze seemed hot, and very intense. "But I don't think it's going to work, Olivia."

3

HER HEART SKIPPED A BEAT and a swelling sensation of near panic threatened to suffocate her. Had she pushed him too far? "You want to call it off?"

"No!" He abandoned his casual pose and was again leaning toward her. "No, I just don't think I'm going to be able to look at this as anything *but* personal. I've thought about it a lot over the past few days and I don't believe it's at all possible to sleep with a woman—a woman I know and admire—and pretend that it isn't the least bit intimate. I do think we can get past that, though, if we both try."

"I'm not sure I understand." At least he wasn't canceling on her, and that was all that really mattered.

"I think we should look at this as something of an adventure. So long as we limit our socializing to the...ah...process, we should be able to keep things in perspective."

"I see. No friendly visits between appointments."

"Exactly. We'll meet when we have to in order to see things through, but the rest of the time our relationship, such as it is, will remain the same."

"Which is strictly business."

"Yes."

Olivia toyed with her fork. For some ridiculous reason she felt insulted. Her tone was a touch acerbic when she remarked, "That serves my purposes just fine. I'll enjoy you while you employ all your manly skills to impregnate me." A mental image formed with her words, and she had to catch her breath. "As to the rest, if you'll recall, I don't have time for frivolous dating."

He curled his hand into a fist and searched her face, looking as if he wanted to say more, but then he shook his head, and said, "All right, we're agreed then. And this weekend is fine for me, also. Should we begin Friday evening?"

"I'll be at the Southend location that day, but I'll finish up about six."

"That's good for me." He reached out to straighten his knife and fork, and Olivia saw that his hand was shaking. She shook, too, in impatience. "I'll make arrangements for us somewhere private, then meet you there. That way, no one will see us together, which I think is important. We need to maintain our social distance."

It was the physical closeness that interested Olivia, not the social distance, so she nodded. "I'd just as soon no one suspected us of enhancing our relationship, too. I don't want to start any nasty gossip and end up in a scandal."

He chuckled. "At least you wouldn't have to worry about your folks catching wind of it. My entire family lives nearby, and they all think they need to straighten

out my life. Anytime the mere hint of a scandal sur-
faces, I find them all at my door ready and willing to
butt right in."

"And what we're conspiring to do goes beyond the
'hint' stage. It *defines* the word scandalous."

"Which means my family would have a field day."

Olivia was fascinated. She'd often wondered what
kind of upbringing Tony had, especially in light of the
fact she had no family at all. He was such a good person, she supposed his family had to be pretty good,
too. "So they have no idea what you're planning? I
mean, with the baby and all?"

"Hell no. My family is old-fashioned. They definitely believe in doing things in the right order."

"Marriage first?"

"Yep." He grinned again, that ready grin that made
all the ladies of his acquaintance smile in yearning.
"They've been very diligent in trying to get me married off. Every damn one of them has produced at least
three prospective brides. I can't make them understand
that I'd prefer to do the choosing myself when I decide
the time is right."

Olivia suddenly realized they'd already broken their
new set of rules. Learning about Tony's family definitely went beyond business and was dangerous besides; the more she knew about him, the more fascinating he seemed. It had taken her no time at all to become
accustomed to wanting him, to accepting him as a desirable man. Every day, every minute it seemed, her
feelings for him grew. She began to wonder if those

feelings hadn't been there all along, waiting to be noticed.

It was a very scary prospect. She couldn't afford, professionally or emotionally, to get overly involved with him. So she changed the subject, away from his family, and tried to dwell on something less intimate.

Their soup was delivered and throughout the rest of the lunch they discussed Olivia's new shop and Tony's proposed agreement. To his credit, Tony argued fiercely, but Olivia wore him down. The meal ended with Tony promising to have his lawyer okay everything and return the finalized papers to her very soon.

They stood on the curb outside the restaurant, the lunchtime crowd flowing around them, and Tony touched her arm. "Friday at six."

"I'll be ready."

He started to move toward his car, then halted and turned back to her. "I hope you know what you've gotten yourself into."

Olivia never wavered. As with all her decisions, she didn't allow room for regrets. She held his gaze and nodded.

"Good. Because I think we'll barely make it inside the door before I'll lose my control. You've pushed a lot on this deal, lady, more than any before. You've demanded that I give you pleasure, and that I spend a great deal of time doing it." He reached up and flicked a finger over her cheek, so very briefly. "Friday night, you're liable to find I have a few demands of my own."

Olivia watched him stride away, and then as a smile

spread over her face, she whispered, "Oh, I do hope so, Tony, I really do."

DISGUSTED WITH HERSELF, Olivia knew she wasn't going to get any real work done. She'd spent Friday afternoon having her legs waxed and her nails manicured, then left the shop early to go home and shower and change. She'd meant to get back in time to do some inventory, but she'd lingered over choosing an outfit, trying to find something simple and attractive, while not wanting to display too obviously her wish to be appealing. By the time she returned to the shop, she had only a little time before Tony was due to pick her up.

After saying good-night to her store manager, she settled down to look over the most recent batch of applications for new jobs, thanks to Tony. She'd already decided to promote one woman to manager of the new store, but then she had to fill that woman's position. Olivia was fortunate in always having found excellent employees. She'd learned from Tony that you got what you paid for, and she'd always been generous with her benefits.

As soon as thoughts of Tony entered her mind, she started daydreaming again. She should have bought a new outfit for today, she thought, looking down at her simple beige wool skirt and matching tunic. The top had a row of pearl buttons that started just above her breasts and ended at the hem. As she imagined Tony undoing those buttons, one by one, she shivered.

She'd tossed aside her normal panty hose in favor of

silky stockings with a pale rose satin garter, a big seller
for the shops. She had even dabbed on perfume in very
naughty places. Her pumps were midheeled and made
her legs extra long and shapely. To balance the effect,
she'd left her hair loose, parted in the middle, and it fell
to rest against the top of her shoulders. She was so nervous, she'd long since chewed off any lipstick she
might have applied, and decided against fussing with
more.

She'd probably feel more confident, she thought, if
she'd worn something daring, something sinful and
sexy. Her selection of underclothes often gave her confidence, especially when no one knew she was wearing
them.

She walked to a rack and picked up a teddy that
fairly screamed enticement with rosette patterns of lace
across the breasts and between the legs. She fingered
the material, feeling it slide through her hands. She
drew in a deep, shuddering breath imagining it sliding
through Tony's hands.

When she heard the bell over the door chime, even
though the Closed sign was up, she jerked, then
quickly spun around to face the door.

Tony walked in, his hands shoved deep into the
pockets of his dress pants, and she could only stare.
His gaze connected with hers, and he started forward
with a steady, determined stride. He didn't stop at the
counter, but came to the rack where she stood, her lips
parted, the teddy still in her hand.

His eyes moved over her, lingering on the teddy, and he asked, "Are we alone here?"

She nodded. "I was just finishing up—"

He laid a finger against her lips. There was no smile on his mouth, no welcome in his eyes. He looked intent and determined and very hungry. He slid his hand into her hair and cupped her head, stepping closer until his pant legs brushed her skirt. And then he kissed her.

IT HAD BEEN WORTH THE WAIT.

He couldn't remember ever feeling so anxious for a woman. It was the teasing, he was certain, that had brought him low. Olivia, in her usual forceful, decisive way, had seduced him most thoroughly. Odd, but he hadn't ever thought of her business manner carrying over into something so personal. He knew so damn little about her personal life.

Such as whether or not she really ever wore a garment as sexy as the teddy in her hand.

That was something he could soon find out. Because it was obvious she used the same tack of gaining what she wanted whether it was business or pleasure. And she wanted him.

That thought had plagued him all week, and it had been all he could do to maintain a touch of control over himself. What he needed, he thought, was a long, hot, intimate evening alone with her. And then he'd be able to get her out of his system and put her, and his purpose for being with her, in proper perspective. But damn, she tasted good.

He knew he should pull back, give her time to catch her breath, but she wasn't fighting him, wasn't behaving in a particularly shocked manner. She merely stood there and gave him free rein. He slanted his mouth over hers again, then lightly coasted his tongue over her bottom lip. She groaned.

Apart from the one hand he had in her hair and his mouth, Tony didn't touch her. Olivia's hands remained at her sides, almost as if she was afraid to move them. He leaned back and stared down at her face. Her dark brown eyes were half closed, the thick lashes seeming to weigh them down. Her lips were still parted, and her cheeks were flushed. He liked that.

"We're going back to my house."

She blinked twice, then cleared her throat. "I assumed you'd rent a place..."

"My home is very private. And I don't want to be running around town. Too many people know me. Besides, today is my birthday. Someone might decide to surprise me with a bottle of champagne or some such nonsense, and once we're alone, I don't want to be disturbed."

Her eyes widened. "Happy birthday. I didn't realize... You should be celebrating with someone special."

He started to tell her she was special, almost too special, but he bit back the words. "It's okay. More than okay." He bent to kiss her very quickly. She looked disappointed when he pulled away. "I can't think of a better way to spend the day. You're giving me the best gift imaginable."

No sooner did he say it, than he realized she might misunderstand. So he quickly clarified, "A baby, I mean."

"I knew what you meant."

But he was lying, to both her and himself. Right now, he wanted her so much, thoughts of conception were taking a back seat to good old-fashioned lust. He still wanted his baby, very much, but he found himself hoping it would take a couple of tries before they found success. He wanted—needed—to expend all his desire for her so he could concentrate on other, more important things.

Olivia looked slightly rattled, which was new for her. She reached behind herself to feel for a hanger, then slipped the teddy onto it and back on the rack. Tony looked around, taking in the ambience of the shop. He'd been in them all, of course, but still, she never ceased to amaze him with her organization and natural ability for merchandising.

She did a remarkable amount of business, and it was easy to see why.

Everything was displayed in a way that bespoke intimacy with a touch of class. Mannequins were shyly posed in every corner, their perfect forms draped in soft pastel shades of silk and satin, musky scents filled the air from the perfume rack and the shelves of sachets. Every inch of space was utilized to the best advantage, so nothing looked crowded or busy.

Olivia cleared her throat, drawing his attention. "I was thinking of ordering more of these," she said, indicating the teddys. "I knew they'd be a big seller, but this week we went through more than even I had anticipated. They're just so comfortable."

"And incredibly sexy?"

She nodded. That Olivia felt the need for small talk proved her nervousness, and Tony didn't want her nervous. He also couldn't stop himself from asking the question of the day. "How do you know they're comfortable, Olivia? Do you wear these things?" He reached over and caught at the lace edging the leg of the teddy, then rubbed his thumb over it.

Straightening her spine, a gesture of defiance he was beginning to recognize, she nodded. "Of course I do. I've personally tried everything I sell."

Tony took another quick survey of the shop, and this time his gaze landed on a midnight black bra and panty set, the bra designed to merely cup the fullness of the breast, leaving the nipples exposed, and the panties with a very convenient open seam. He felt his stomach constrict, and knew he had to get her out of the shop before his libido exploded. "Are you ready to go?"

Appearing as flustered as he felt, she nodded and reached behind the counter for her coat. Tony helped her slip it on, then took her arm to guide her out. She was trembling, and he wanted to reassure her somehow, but as she locked up the shop, he saw that her nipples were peaked against the soft wool of her tunic, and any coherent conversation escaped him. He wanted to touch her breasts, to see if they felt as soft as they looked. He wanted to taste her, all of her, and he wanted to give her the pleasure she'd requested.

At first, it had seemed like a tall order, and a bit intimidating. No woman had ever come right out and told him to give her the level of satisfaction she expected. It was enough to shrivel many a man. But he wasn't a man to cower under pressure, and the more he'd thought of it—and ways to see the job done—the more excited he'd become by the prospect. Going head-to-head with Olivia during business always exhilarated him. Doing so in bed would be even better. He felt challenged for the first time in a long time, and what red-blooded male could resist a challenge?

Besides, he decided, as they drove from the parking garage, if he didn't get it right the first time, he'd have plenty of time to keep trying. That thought brought a grin.

"What?"

He glanced at Olivia and realized she was watching him. She looked wary now, and a little self-conscious. "Hey, you're not having second thoughts, are you?"

"No, but I'll admit that grin of yours is a little unnerving."

He heard the slight tremor in her tone and reached over to take her hand from her lap. "I'm just..."

"Eager?"

"That's a very appropriate word." He grinned again. "What about you?"

She drew a quavering breath, then whispered, "Yes."

Tony had to put both hands on the wheel. Never had one simple word affected him so strongly. He wanted to speed, to race to his house, but the streets were congested with holiday shoppers. With Thanksgiving less than two weeks away, it seemed as if everyone had a reason to be out on a Friday evening. Curse them all.

"How far do we have to go?"

"It's about a twenty-minute drive." Twenty minutes that would seem like two hours. "Are you hungry?"

"No."

"Are you sure? I could stop at a drive-through."

She glared at him. "No. I am not hungry."

He liked the idea that she was as anxious to get under way as he. They stopped at a traffic light and he said, "Well, then how about scooting over here and giving me another kiss? It's the truth, I desperately need something to tide me over."

Her chest rose and fell in several deep breaths, then she scooted. Tony caught her mouth, pressing her back against the seat and this time skipping the teasing. He slid his tongue into her mouth and stroked her deeply. Olivia's hands came up to rest on his shoulders, and then curled to pull him closer.

The light changed, and at a snail's pace, traffic moved.

They continued to kiss and cuddle and touch at

every opportunity, and Tony knew they were making each other just a bit crazy. But he didn't call a halt to the touching, and finally, after excruciating frustration, he pulled into his long driveway. It had taken twenty-five minutes, and every minute had been a form of inventive foreplay. Olivia had her eyes closed and appeared to be concentrating on breathing. Her coat laid open, her knees pressed tightly together, and her hands, where they rested on the seat on either side of her, shook.

Tony said very softly, "We're here."

She slowly sat forward and surveyed his home through bleary eyes. She was quiet for long seconds, then whispered, "Oh, Tony. It's beautiful."

He was pleased with her praise. "I had it built a few years ago. I made certain as many trees were left as possible."

"It almost seems a part of the landscape."

That had been his intention. Built of stone and wood and slate, the house blended in with the background, sprawling wide with only one level, and surrounded by oaks and pines and dogwoods. "Now, with the trees bare, you can see the house better. But in the spring and summer, it's nearly hidden."

He hit the remote to open the garage door, then drove inside. The four-car garage held only one other car, and was very quiet.

When he opened Olivia's door for her and she stepped out, he couldn't help but kiss her again. And this time, since they were assured of privacy, he gave his eager hands the freedom to roam. His palms coasted over her back, feeling her warmth even through the thickness of her coat, then scooped low to cuddle her soft rounded buttocks.

Olivia sucked in a deep breath and moaned when he brought her flush with his body. He knew she could feel his erection, knew she was reacting to it, and with every rapid pulse beat of his body, he thought: this is Olivia, the cool businesswoman, the shark, and she's pressing against me, trembling and wanting more. It was wonderful and strange and so exciting he almost couldn't bear it. He felt his body harden even more, felt himself expanding, growing. He felt ready to burst.

He back-stepped her toward the door leading into his house. Now that he was this close, he certainly didn't want to make love to her in the garage. But when he lifted his head, his eyes were immediately drawn to her heaving breasts, and he saw again her stiff little nipples. Her coat was open down the front, and he pushed it further aside, then gently cupped her breasts, shaping them, weighing them in his palms. She was soft and warm and her nipples were pressed achingly against the fabric. She tilted her head back against the garage wall and made a small sound of pleasure and need.

Before he could give his mind time to approve his actions, he unbuttoned three small pearl buttons, and peeled aside the soft wool material. Her bra was lace and satin, a pale coffee color, but so sheer he could see the entire outline of her. It nearly sent him over the edge. He brushed his thumb over her nipple, gently, teasing, and watched her tremble. He lost control.

He growled low in his throat, pulled the bra down so it was cupped beneath her pale breast, pushing her up, seeming to offer her to his mouth, and then he brushed his thumb over her again. She panted as he toyed with her, building the suspense, the excitement.

"Tony."

It was her small, pleading voice that brought him around. He couldn't wait much longer to taste her, but neither should he be rushing things. He kept his eyes on her beautiful body, on the breast he'd bared, then wrapped his arm around her waist to guide her inside. He reached for the doorknob and turned it, then jerked when he heard a screamed, *"Surprise!"*

He looked up and saw his entire family, balloons in the background, streamers floating around. It took everyone a second to realize the misfortune of the entire scene, and then little by little, expressions changed. He saw his mother gasp, his grandfather chuckle. His brother was now wearing a wide grin.

His own face must have looked stunned, and he couldn't find the wherewithal to move. Both he and Olivia seemed frozen to the spot. Then he saw his six-year-old nephew turn his gaze to Olivia, and watched as his sister-in-law rushed over and slapped both hands over her son's eyes. Tony came reluctantly to his senses. He slammed the door shut, then tried to get his mind to function in some semblance of order so he could figure out what to do.

"Oh my God."

He glanced down at Olivia, her hands covering her face, her shoulders shaking. She said again, "Oh my God." Her breast was still uncovered, and more than anything, he wanted to taste that small pink nipple. He wished his family elsewhere, but when he heard the sudden roar of hysterical laughter inside, he knew not a single damn one of them would budge. Meddling bunch of irritants.

"Oh my God."

Tony frowned, his gaze still on that taunting nipple. He was beginning to feel like Pavlov's dog. "Are you praying or cursing?"

She peeked at him from between her fingers, her expression as evil as any he'd ever seen. Through gritted teeth, she said, "You promised me privacy, Tony. There must be fifty people in there."

"No. If everyone's present, and I suspect by the low roar that they are, there's ten, maybe twelve total. It only seems like more because a portion of them are kids. Noisy kids." She dropped her hands and glared at him. She seemed totally oblivious to the fact that her body was bared. Tony, still retaining a death grip on the doorknob in case anyone tried to open it, reached over to cup her with his free hand. She jerked.

"*Tony.*"

How her voice could change from cold and angry to soft and pleading so quickly, he didn't know. "One small taste, Olivia, okay? Then I can sort the rest of this out."

She didn't appear to understand, which was probably the only reason she didn't protest.

Tony shook his head, then bent down and slowly drew his tongue around her nipple. She gasped, and he gently sucked her into his mouth, holding her captive with his teeth. Her flesh was hot and sweet and her nipple was so taut it pained him. He licked his tongue over her, flicking, teasing, making her nipple strain even more. When she moaned, he suckled, holding her close to his body.

Olivia's hands settled in his hair just as a discreet knock sounded on the door. "You might as well come in, Tony. I sent the kids into the kitchen for some punch."

Tony cursed, dropped his forehead to Olivia's chest, then felt himself rudely pushed aside as she frantically tried to right her bra and button herself up. "Calm down, Olivia, it's all right."

From the other side of the door, he heard his brother say, "Yeah, Olivia. It's all right. We're glad you're here for the party."

Tony growled. "Go away, John!"

"All right. But I'll be back in two minutes if you don't present yourself. Both of you."

Now that she was decently covered, Olivia sent her gaze searching around the garage, and Tony realized she was hoping to find a means of escape. "Forget it. They won't let me leave, therefore, you're stuck, too."

"But you don't want this," she wailed, her hands twisting together at her waist. "This is your family,

Tony, part of your private life, and I don't want to intrude. We both agreed I wouldn't intrude."

Tony sighed, knowing she was right, but also accepting the inevitable. "I'll find some way to throw my family off the scent. Just play it cool. As far as they need to know, we're business associates and nothing more."

Olivia's look told him how stupid she thought that idea was. "Play it cool? After what they saw us doing?" She shook her head. "No. I'm not going in there."

"Olivia..."

"They *saw* us!"

He shrugged. "It's none of their damn business. If anyone gets impertinent with you, tell them to bug off. Or better still, just tell me, and I'll handle them."

She didn't look at all convinced, and Tony touched her face. "I've seen you at work, lady. You can easily handle a few curious relatives. You're a shark, remember? Now pull yourself together."

She drew a deep breath and gave an uncertain nod. Tony dropped his gaze to her mouth, then had to swallow a curse. His fingertips slid over her lower lip. "Do you have any idea how frustrated I am right now? How badly I'm hurting?"

Olivia seemed to regain some of her aplomb. "No more than I am, I assume. After all, this was my idea. You, as I recall, were very reluctant to agree."

"I was an idiot." He turned to the door again. "I suppose I can suffer through a few hours. How long can a family birthday party last anyway?"

OLIVIA TRIED for a serene smile as Tony's family lined up to meet her. Tony waited until he had everyone's attention, then said with astounding sincerity, "Everyone, this is Olivia Anderson. She's a business associate. She owns the lingerie shops Sugar and Spice in the hotels, and today we were working on finalizing the placement of one more."

Olivia held her breath, but no one called him on the obvious cover-up. Then Tony began pointing out people, too many of them for Olivia to keep straight, though she was usually very good with names and faces. The men seemed inclined to leave her be, their interest caught by a football game someone had turned on. Other than a wave in her direction when Tony introduced her, and a few ribald comments to Tony and the kind of *business* he conducted, they stayed on or near the family-room couch and the large-screen television.

The women, however, hovered. They were anxious to talk to her, and Tony, with little more than an apologetic glance, abandoned her when the men called him to watch a play. Sue, Tony's mother, invited her to join the women and children in the kitchen.

To Olivia's surprise, no one was the least bit unpleasant, despite what had happened. "I'm sorry if we've upset your plans," Sue said. "Tony, of course, didn't know we'd planned a party. And we didn't know Tony had made other arrangements."

Tony's sister, Kate, and sister-in-law, Lisa, both chuckled. Kate said, "If you could have seen his face! Well, we certainly did surprise him."

Olivia couldn't help but smile. Both women were very adept at keeping busy in the kitchen, and dodging the kids who ran in and out. "It was rather awkward."

Lisa laughed. "For us, too. Of course, John is just like Tony, and never lets a chance go by to goad his brother."

"And they both goad me. Endlessly!" Kate shook her head. "But now I have enough ammunition to twit Tony for a good month."

Olivia decided, even though their comments weren't malicious, it was time to change the subject. She didn't want to have to explain her business with Tony. "Could I help you do something?"

Sue was arranging ham slices on a platter, Kate was putting glasses and napkins on a tray, and Lisa was trying to balance a tiny infant in one arm and dish up potato salad with the other. She turned with a relieved smile when Olivia made her offer.

"If you wouldn't mind holding the baby, that would be a big help."

Olivia balked. "I, uh, how about I help with the food instead? I've never held an infant before."

"Piece of cake, believe me. And he's such a good baby, he won't give you any problems."

Before Olivia could form another denial, the baby

was nestled in her arms. His mother had wrapped him in a soft blue blanket, and other than one tiny hand and a small, pink face, the child was completely covered. Olivia cuddled him carefully when he squirmed, settling himself with a small sigh that parted his pursed lips and made Olivia smile.

She felt a pain in her chest that had nothing to do with physical ailments and everything to do with a breaking heart.

One by one, the women left the kitchen to carry the trays into the dining room, and Olivia welcomed the privacy. She couldn't recall ever holding such a small baby before, and her curiosity was extreme. She carefully pushed the blanket back from the baby's head, then rubbed her cheek against his crown. So soft, she thought, wondering at the silky cap of hair. And the scents. Never had she smelled anything so sweet, so touching, as a baby. She wanted to breathe his scent all day. She had her nose close to him, gently nuzzling him, when Tony walked in.

"What are you doing?"

Olivia jerked at the alarm in his tone. She didn't have time to answer him, though, not that she would have told him she was smelling the baby. Lisa came back in then and thanked her. "I'll put him in his crib now that the other kids are all sitting down to eat. I worry when they're all running around that they'll wake him up. You know how kids are."

Olivia didn't know, but she could see Tony hadn't liked her holding the baby. Lisa left the room, and

Tony whispered, "Do you think it's a good idea for you to do that?"

Olivia knew exactly what he meant. He was concerned she'd start wanting a baby herself if she held one. She could have told him it was too late for that worry, that it didn't matter. She could want forever and never get what she wished. At least, she couldn't get a baby. Now passion, it seemed Tony was ready to give her that in huge doses. What she'd felt during the ride and in his garage... It was almost everything she'd ever wanted with a man. Everything but the real emotion. Everything but love.

It angered her that he was pushing her and worrying about something that would never be, but she held in her words of resentment and instead, she shrugged. "Would you have rather I'd refused? What excuse would I give?"

He tunneled his fingers through his hair, then looked toward the dining room. "Come on. They're waiting for me to eat."

"This is going to be impossible, isn't it, Tony?"

"No. Everything's fine."

He didn't sound at all convincing, and Olivia had to wonder if John or Kate had already been teasing him. When they entered the dining room, Olivia looked around. She hadn't had the chance to actually see the inside of Tony's house, but now that she could look, she wasn't at all surprised. Everything, every dish, every piece of furniture, the wallpaper, all showed excellent taste, but without the blatant stamp of wealth.

Tony never flaunted his financial success, and other than the size of the sprawling house, it showed only a sense of comfort and functional ease.

The house was very open. Each room seemed to flow into the next, and there were windows everywhere. The furniture was all highly polished mahogany. As little Maggie, who Olivia guessed to be around three, walked to her seat with one hand on the buffet, she left small smudge marks in her wake. Tony only scooped her up and tossed her in the air. The little girl giggled, wrapped her pudgy arms around Tony's neck and planted a very wet kiss on the side of his nose. He pretended to chew on her belly, then sat her in her booster seat and took his own chair next to Olivia. The rest of the children yelled for his attention.

The pain in her chest intensified.

She so desperately wanted this one sumptuous, sensuous affair. The whole purpose was to help her fill a void, because her life was destined to be a lonely one, without children and without a man who loved her. But she was getting more than she bargained for. She hadn't wanted to be shown all she was missing, to find more voids, to have first-hand knowledge of what could never be hers.

As she watched Tony laugh and play with the children, she knew it was too late for her. Perhaps this would yet turn out to be the wild fling she'd anticipated, but it would also leave her lonelier than ever before.

Dinner was a wonderful, riotous affair with children

laughing, grown-ups talking and food being continuously resupplied. The kids quickly realized Olivia was a new face and, therefore, easy to entertain. Despite her growing melancholy, she laughed at their antics, listened to their stories, and when one child came over and tugged on her skirt, she didn't even flinch over the stain left behind. The child wanted to be lifted, and Olivia obliged. But the small hand was still holding her skirt, and when the child went up, so did her hem.

She hurried to right herself, pushing her skirt back down. But it was obvious everyone had seen the top of her stocking and the paler strip of flesh on her upper thigh. John grinned, Lisa gave him a playful smack to keep him from speaking, and Sue quickly began talking about Christmas shopping.

Olivia glanced at Tony and saw he had his eyes closed, looking close to prayer. Despite his brother's chuckles, it took him a few moments to collect his control. And then he sent Olivia a smile that made promises and threats at the same time.

After that, Tony did his best to deflect the kids from her. Olivia understood his reasoning, but no one else did. And all in all, everyone accepted her. They attempted to make her a part of their family, and for the short while it could last, Olivia loved it. Every few minutes, someone stood to check on the sleeping infant, whose crib they could see in the family room through the archway. The men took more turns than the women did, and Olivia saw that Tony, more than anyone, was interested in peeking in on the little one.

Olivia was being smothered by the sense of familial camaraderie. As welcoming as they all were, she felt like an interloper. And when she spied the pile of gaily wrapped birthday presents in the corner, she knew she couldn't stay.

She excused herself, asking directions to the powder room, then quickly located a phone. It happened to be in Tony's bedroom, or so she assumed judging from the open closet door and the lingering scent of his cologne...and his body. Again, she found herself breathing deeply, then shook her head and forced her mind to clear. She perched on the side of the bed to call for a cab.

She was still sitting there minutes later when Tony found her.

4

TONY SLIPPED into the room and quietly closed the door. Olivia looked up and their gazes touched, hers wide, his narrowed. He crossed his arms over his chest and kept his voice very low. "Hiding?"

"What do you think?"

"No. I don't think you'd hide. So what are you doing?"

Olivia came to her feet, feeling like a fool, like a sneaky fool. But she refused to be intimidated. "I called a cab. I think it's past time I went home."

Tony didn't say anything at first, just leaned back against the door. Then he closed his eyes and groaned. "You're going to make me wait another day, aren't you, Olivia?"

Her heartbeat jumped at the husky way he said that, and at the restrained hunger she heard in his tone. "This...this isn't the right time, Tony. You know that. Right now, I feel equal parts ridiculous and embarrassed."

His gaze pinned her, hot and intent. "I could make you forget your hesitation real fast, honey."

I'll just bet you could. It wasn't easy, but Olivia shook

her head. "If I leave now, they might not suspect anything—"

"Olivia, they saw me kissing your breast. I think they're already a bit suspicious."

She felt the blood pound in her veins, but kept her gaze steady. "You weren't kissing my breast."

"I wanted to be."

Olivia curled her hands into fists and tried to calm her breathing. "They might decide that was just a temporary loss of control if I leave now. If I stay until they're all gone, they'll assume we're spending the night together, and that's what we wanted to avoid." She gentled her tone and asked, "No speculation, no gossip. No scandals. Remember?"

"Yeah, but—"

A knock sounded at the door, and John's jovial voice called out, "Everything okay in there?"

Tony closed his eyes, a look of annoyance etched in his features. "I'm going to kill him."

Olivia thought she might help.

"We'll be out in just a second, John. And if you dare knock on the damn door again, I'm going to knock on you."

"Hey! I just wanted to tell you they're ready to cut the cake."

"So you told me. Now disappear, will you?"

Olivia rubbed her forehead, knowing she'd fumbled again, that she'd only made matters worse. Good grief, Tony's brother was fetching them from the bedroom.

"How that man produced such a beautiful, sweet baby, I don't know."

To her surprise, Tony laughed. "John's all right. Believe me, if he understood the situation, he wouldn't be hassling me."

"No?"

Tony slowly shook his head, then went to her and pulled her against his chest. "No. He'd be sympathetic as hell." He tilted her head back and growled, "I want you, Olivia."

Her stomach curled at his words. "Tomorrow?"

Tony placed damp kisses across her cheek, her throat. He touched the corner of her mouth with his tongue. "Early? You're not going to make me wait until evening, are you?"

Olivia thought she might agree to anything with him stroking her back and kissing her so softly. "Where?"

"Hell, I don't know. But I'll think of something before morning, okay? I'll pick you up. About ten o'clock?"

"That'll be fine." She forced herself to forget how sensual and romantic everything seemed with Tony, and to concentrate on their purpose. She had to keep in mind that this was temporary, that Tony didn't really want her, not for keeps. He only wanted to use her, just as she would use him. "I don't want you to worry, Tony. We still have time. I'm supposed to be very fertile for the next couple of days."

She'd barely finished with the words before he was giving her a real kiss, his tongue moving against her own, his teeth nipping. It was a kiss meant to last her through the night. Unfortunately she could still feel the heat in her cheeks when she was forced to walk back into the dining room. She was grateful that the lights had been turned out, and the candles on the cake were lit. She saw John standing by the light switch and knew he was responsible for the darkness. John gave Tony a wink, and Olivia decided he might not be so bad after all.

Kate's two girls, Angie and Allison, ages four and five, fought over who could sing the loudest during the requisite Happy Birthday, and John's son, six-year-old Luke, wanted to cut and serve the cake. Though Olivia explained that she had to leave, they all insisted she eat a piece of cake first and enjoy a scoop of ice cream. Olivia couldn't remember the last time she'd had, or attended, a birthday party. It might have been fun today if she'd actually been a part of it, rather than a reluctant intruder.

She didn't want anyone to know she'd called a cab. She thought it might seem less awkward if everyone thought she was driving herself home, so she had her coat on and her purse in her hand when she saw the cab's lights coming down the long driveway. To her surprise, the kids all wanted to give her hugs goodbye, the parents all uttered enthusiastic wishes to see her again soon, and to her chagrin, Tony's mother invited her to Thanksgiving dinner. Olivia muttered a lame, "Thank you, but I'll have to see," along with something about a busy schedule, and then she rushed out the door, wanting only to escape the onslaught of emotions. Tony caught her on the last step of the porch.

"I'm sorry, Olivia. I know this wasn't easy for you." He glanced at the cab and cursed. "I should be driving you home."

"I don't mind the cab, Tony, and you can't very well leave your own birthday party."

He reached for his wallet, and she narrowed her eyes. "What do you think you're doing?"

"At least let me pay for the cab—"

"Absolutely not and I won't hear another word on it." She used her most inflexible tone, the one that got contracts altered and had suppliers promising early deliveries. "I'm not your responsibility."

His sigh was long and filled with irritation. "Will you do me a favor then, and at least call me when you get home?"

Olivia stared. She was used to taking care of herself and his request seemed more than absurd. "Why?"

"So I know you made it home okay."

"Tony, you can't start feeling responsible for me. That's breaking one of the rules, isn't it? I'm a big girl, and I know how to manage on my own. So don't worry."

"Call me."

He was insistent, using his own invaluable, corporate tone, and she could tell by his stubborn stance he wasn't going to relent. She didn't think it was a good idea, but she gave in anyway. "Okay. But only this once."

"Thanks." He was grinning hugely.

"You're not a gracious winner, Tony."

"I haven't won yet. Hell, I've still got a whole room full of relatives who are going to burst with rapid-fire questions as soon as I step back inside. Now that you're gone and therefore can't be offended, they'll revert to their normal unrestrained selves."

She knew he was teasing, knew he was very close to his family, and for that reason she suffered not a single twinge of guilt for leaving him to his fate. She stepped into the cab, and Tony came to lean inside, ignoring the cabdriver and giving her a quick kiss.

"Tomorrow, Olivia. Then I'll win."

He was taunting her, but she only grinned. It was in her nature to give as good as she got, so when he started to pull away, she caught his neck and drew him back for another kiss, this one much longer and hotter than the first. And while he was trying to catch his breath, she whispered, "We'll both win."

Tony chuckled. But as he stepped away from the cab, they both looked up. And there at the front door, huddled together as if for a kindergarten class picture, stood all of Tony's family. And even with only the moon for light, Olivia could see the wide grins on all their faces.

TONY GLANCED AT THE CLOCK, but it was only seven in the morning, and he had no real reason to get up, not when he wouldn't be seeing Olivia until ten. So he lingered in bed, thinking about her, about all that had happened the night before. Her vulnerability around his family stirred feelings he didn't want to acknowledge—especially when concentrating on the lust she engendered was so much more satisfying.

Not one single minute had passed during the night when he could completely put Olivia and her allure from his mind. It was ridiculous, but he wanted her more now than he'd ever wanted any woman. Of course, she was so different from any other woman he knew. She made demands, but she also gave freely of herself. She was a veritable shark whenever they did business, but she ran her business fairly, and with a generous hand toward her workers. It was a belief he subscribed to: Treat your employees honestly, and you get honesty and loyalty in return.

They actually had a lot in common.

And yet there was a multitude of reasons why he couldn't get overly involved with her. The very things he admired about her made her most unsuitable for an emotional relationship. He wanted a baby, pure and simple, someone to love him, and someone he could love without restrictions or qualifications. The baby would be his, only his, and Tony planned to smother the child with all the love he had inside him.

Olivia wanted a thriving business. She'd admitted she had no desire, no time for a family. She'd agreed to have his baby as part of a business deal, and while her agreement thrilled him, it also reemphasized the fact that business was still her main objective in life, while a baby was now his. He'd have to do his best to remember that.

The house was chilly when he finally rose and went to put on coffee. Naked except for a pair of snug cotton boxers, he felt the gooseflesh rise on his arms, but he ignored it. He needed a little cooling off if he was to deal with Olivia in a rational way.

He went into the bathroom and splashed water over his beard-rough face, then brushed his teeth while he waited for the coffee. Today, he thought, staring at his own contemplative expression in the mirror, he would get this business with Olivia back on an even keel. No more mingling with family, no more seeing her with a baby cuddled in her arms and an expression on her face that tore at his guts. He would view her with a detached eye and a reminder in his brain that she was a means to an end. They'd made an agreement, and it could be nothing more.

Not if he expected to escape this ordeal completely intact, with his heart whole and his mind sane.

He'd just poured his first cup of coffee when the doorbell rang. Padding barefoot into the living room, he leaned down to peer through the peephole and saw Olivia standing on his doorstep. A quick glance at the clock showed it to be only seven forty-five, and his first thought was that she was here to cancel, that something had come up and she had to go out of town; it wasn't uncommon in her business. Every muscle in his body protested.

He jerked the door open, forgetting for the moment

that he wasn't even close to being dressed. Olivia took a long moment to stare at his chest, then down the length of his body before she lifted her gaze to his face.

"You're rather hairy, aren't you?"

"I'll shave."

Her lips quirked in a quick grin. "Your chest?"

If it would keep her from canceling. He only shrugged.

Tentatively she reached out and touched him, laying her palm flat where his heart beat in unsteady cadence. She stroked him, feeling him, tangling her fingers in his body hair. With a breathless whisper, she said, "I like it."

Tony didn't answer. He wasn't certain he could answer. And then she looked up at him, her eyes huge and bright. "I couldn't wait."

He felt the bottom drop out of his stomach. His hand shook as he set the cup of coffee on the entry table, then reached for her and pulled her inside. He needed to make certain he'd understood. "Olivia?"

She started to chatter. "I know you said ten, but we're both off today, right? And I'm really not used to this, being aroused and yet having to wait. It's terribly difficult. I couldn't sleep last night..."

"Me, either."

He couldn't believe she was here, looking shy and determined and he wanted her as much as he'd ever wanted anything in his life. Everything he'd just been telling himself about keeping his emotional distance vanished. He couldn't quite pry his hands from her shoulders, couldn't force himself to take an emotional step back. He felt her softness beneath the coat, the way she straightened her shoulders to face him. Ah, that small show of bravado, so like her, so endearing. So damn sexy.

The brisk morning air coming through the open door did little to impress him. As he felt himself harden, his pulse quicken, Olivia pushed the door shut behind her, then set an overnight bag on the floor. His gaze dropped to it, and she rushed to explain. "I... Well, I felt a little risqué this morning. And it stands to reason your house should be safe now. I mean, lightning doesn't strike twice in the same spot, right?"

He had no answer for that, not when he could see the heated need in her eyes, the way her lips trembled.

She swallowed hard. "I don't want you to think I'm intruding for the whole night, but I needed to bring something to wear for later... If we're going to spend the whole day together."

Before he could reassure her, she shook her head and started again, her tone anxious. "I'm making a mess of this. Remember, the book said we should wait a few hours then try again, and I thought..."

"Shh." He could barely restrain himself from lifting her and carrying her to his room. She had this strange mix of timidity and boldness that made him crazy with wanting. "Let me shower real quick and..."

"No." She shook her head and her dark hair fell over her shoulders, looking soft and silky. "I've waited long enough, Tony. I don't want to wait a single second more."

She was staring down at his body, her gaze resting on his blatant erection clearly defined within his soft cotton boxers. Another quarter inch, one more soft sound from her, and the boxers wouldn't cover him at all. He wanted her to touch him, he wanted... Feeling desperate, he said, "I have to at least shave, honey. I don't want to scratch you."

For a reply, she began unbuttoning her coat, and as each button slid free, his heartbeat accelerated. First he saw soft pale flesh; her throat, her upper chest, the gentle swells of her breasts. But as the coat began to part, he realized she wasn't dressed at all, that she was covered only by the teddy he'd admired the day before in her shop.

He'd had to know, he thought frantically, staring at her body, more perfect than any mannequin. She had a gentle grace that was made to wear such feminine items. He'd questioned whether she really wore the articles she carried, and now she'd proven to him that she did—with perfection. And suddenly it was too much.

Gripping the lapels of the coat in his fists, he shoved it over her shoulders and let it fall free to land unnoticed on the floor, abruptly ending her slow unveiling. Drawn by the sight of her, cheeks flushed, eyes anxious, he scooped her into his arms. He felt her slender thighs against his forearm, her soft breasts against his chest, her lips touching his throat, and he groaned. The bedroom was definitely too far away and he took three long steps to the living-room couch and landed there with her tucked close to his side. His mouth was on hers before she could protest, if that had been her intent. And his hands began exploring every soft swell and heated hollow. He moved too fast, he knew it, but he couldn't seem to stop himself.

She shuddered when his palm smoothed over her silky bottom, sliding between her buttocks, exploring her from behind. He dipped between her thighs to frantically finger the three small silver snaps there. They easily popped free at his prodding, and then his fingers were touching her warmth, gliding over softly swelled flesh, over crisp feminine curls. He stroked, feeling her wetness, her growing heat. The feel of her made him wonder why he didn't explode. He could hear her rapid breathing in his ears, feel her fingertips clenching tight on his shoulders.

He groaned, moving his mouth from hers, wanting to taste her skin, to breathe in her scent. She was soft everywhere, from her loose hair that brushed over his cheeks, to her arms that held him tight, to her slender thighs that willingly parted as he continued to cautiously explore her, exciting her, readying her.

Finding a puckered nipple beneath the sheer material of the teddy, he dampened it with his tongue, then looked at his handiwork. She showed pink and erect through the material. He suckled, flicking with his tongue, and Olivia arched her back, her panting, urgent breaths driving him on. He nipped and she gasped. With his big hand still between her thighs, he slid one long finger over her, again and again, finding her most sensitive flesh and plying it in much the same way he did her nipple, then pressing deep inside her, stroking. She made a high, keening sound. She was tight and wet and so hot Tony couldn't stand it another moment; he knew she was ready.

With frenzied motions, he shoved his shorts down and situated himself between her thighs. For one moment, their gazes met, and her look, that unique look of vulnerability and need and demand, pushed him over the edge. He covered her mouth with his own, thrusting his tongue past her lips just as his erection pressed inside her body.

There was a small amount of resistance as her body slowly loosened to accept his length, his size. And then with one even, rough thrust he slid deep, and even that, something beyond her control, appealed to him, made him that much more anxious to reach his final goal. He began moving, driving into her and then pulling away, hearing her panting breaths and feeling the way she tried to counter his moves, though the couch didn't allow her much freedom. He felt things he'd never felt before, as if he were a predatory animal, dominant, determined to stake a primal claim.

Pinning her beneath him so she couldn't move, he slid one hand beneath her hips and lifted, forcing her to take all of him, giving her no way to resist him at all. He briefly worried when she groaned raggedly, but then she squeezed him tight, her muscles clamping around him like a hot fist, and she was slick and wet and she wanted him—wanted him enough to demand that he make love to her. His explosive climax obliterated all other thought.

He knew he shouted like a wild man, knew Olivia watched him with a fascinated type of awe. He threw his head back, sensations continuing to wash over him, draining him, filling him, making his muscles quiver until finally, after long seconds, he collapsed onto her, gasping for breath.

Her arms gently, hesitantly slipped around his neck and her fingers smoothed through his hair. And when he felt the light brushing of her lips over his temple, a touch so unbelievably sweet and innocent, he came to the realization that he'd just used her very badly, that he'd totally ignored all her stipulations of the deal they'd made. He'd forgotten all about the damn deal. Hell, he hadn't given her pleasure.

He hadn't given her anything except a man's lust.

OLIVIA FELT TONY TENSE, knew what was going through his mind, and tightened her arms. He relented enough that he stayed very close to her, but lifted his head. She felt ridiculously shy about meeting his gaze, but she forced herself to do just that, if for no other reason than to reassure him. She couldn't quite prevent the small smile curling her lips.

He blew out a disgusted breath. "I'm sorry."

Placing two fingers against his mouth, she meant only to silence him. But then he kissed her fingers, and her heart flipped and she ended up lifting her own head enough to kiss him in return. "Don't ruin this for me by making unnecessary apologies, Tony. Please."

She said the words against his mouth, and before she'd even finished, his tongue was stroking hers, his narrow, muscular pelvis pushing close again. She tingled all over, a renewed rush of warmth making her stomach curl.

"I already ruined things, honey. And you deserve much more than an apology."

That was the second time he'd called her "honey" and she loved it. There had never been a relationship in her life since her parents' death that warranted an endearment. She hadn't realized that she'd even been missing it. But hearing Tony say it now, hearing the gentleness in his tone, the affection, she decided she liked it very much.

Since he seemed determined to talk about it, Olivia asked, "Why exactly are you apologizing?"

"Because I lost my head. I gave you nothing."

"Not true." Oh how she loved feeling his hard, lean body pressed against hers, the contrast of his firm muscles and his hair-roughened legs and his warmth. She tightened her arms and rubbed her nose against his chest, loving his morning musky scent. He always smelled so good, so sexy. So like himself. It made her dizzy and weak to breathe his delicious scent. "I've never made anyone lose their head before, Tony. I think it's a rather nice feeling."

He gave a strangled laugh, then tangled his hands in

her hair to make her look at him. "I'll take the blame, especially given the fact I've never made love to a woman without a condom before. Feeling you, Olivia, all of you, was a heady experience."

She felt stunned by his admission. "Never?"

"Nope. I've always been the cautious sort, even when I was just a kid. But you're to blame just a bit, too, showing up here in that getup." He ran one large palm down her side, rubbing the material that was now bunched at her waist. His voice dropped to a low rumble when he whispered, "I almost died when you opened your coat, and I knew I wouldn't be able to draw another breath without getting inside you first."

And he thought he hadn't given her anything? With her heart racing and her throat tight with emotion, she kissed him again, getting quickly used to the feel of his mouth on hers. When he lifted his head this time, she was very aware of his renewed erection and the way his arms were taut with muscles as he restrained himself, holding his chest away from her.

Tony watched her so closely, it was hard to speak, but she forced the words out, for some strange reason, wanting to tell him her thoughts. "I was half afraid you'd laugh, that I'd look ridiculous. Though I love wearing sexy things, no one sees me as a sexy woman."

"You're sexier than any woman has a right to be."

"Tony..." The things he said made her light-headed.

"It'll be our little secret, okay?" He began tracing the small red marks left behind from his morning whiskers. That long finger moved over her throat, her breasts. He stopped at her nipples and lightly pinched, holding her between his finger and thumb. He watched her face as he tugged gently, plucking, rolling her flesh until she groaned. Olivia wanted nothing more than to make love with him again.

But Tony was suddenly lifting himself away. "I have to shower and shave," he said in deep, husky tones. "Despite what you say, I don't like leaving burns on your skin."

"No." She tried to protest, to hold him near, but he only stood up then lifted her again. The way he cradled her close to his heart was something else she could get used to.

"You can shower with me, Miss Anderson, then I'll see about attending you the right way."

"I loved the way you did things."

"You didn't come."

A flash of heat washed over her mostly naked body. He had such a blatant way of discussing things that excited her despite her embarrassment. "I... I enjoyed myself." She sounded defensive and added, "But I'm supposed to stay still for a while."

"I can promise you'll enjoy yourself more when I do things properly."

He seemed determined to fulfill her demands, when she now felt horrible for having made them. She didn't want this to be only about base satisfaction, a series of touches meant to excite, with no emotion involved. It was the emotion that she'd been craving for so long, that felt so good now. But there was no way she could say that to Tony, not after she'd told him she wanted to be privy to his excellent technique.

An idea came to mind, and as he stood her inside the shower stall, she said, "Aren't we supposed to wait two hours before doing this again? To give you time to...to replenish yourself?"

Tony stepped in behind her and began working the teddy up over her shoulders. When he finally tossed it outside the shower and stood looking at her completely bare, Olivia knew he'd have his way. He took a long time scrutinizing her, and that gave her a chance to look her fill also. He was such a gorgeous man, so solid, his body dark, his muscles tight.

She wondered if he enjoyed the sight of her near as much as she did him, but then he met her gaze and there was such heat in his green eyes, and more emotion than she could ever wish for, she forgot her own questions.

Tony inched closer to her until their bodies were touching from the waist down. His hard erection pressed into her belly, stealing her breath. His hands came up to cup her breasts. "You don't have to watch the clock, honey. I promise you, it'll take me at least that long to get my fill of looking at you and touching you."

Her heart thumped heavily and she could barely talk. "Tony?"

"It's called foreplay, Olivia. I intend to make up for the orgasm you missed—and then some. We've got all the time in the world."

Thirty minutes later, their still damp bodies tangled in the covers on his bed, Olivia knew she'd never survive two hours worth of this. Tony was gently lathing one nipple while his fingers were busy drifting over her hip and belly, pausing every so often for an excruciating moment between her thighs to torment and tease her until she groaned and begged. He used her own wetness as a lubricant, sometimes pressing his fingers deep, stretching her, other times circling her opening, sliding over ultrasensitive flesh.

He laughed at her soft demands, his fingers gently plucking, rolling. "Easy, sweetheart. I promise, you'll appreciate being patient."

"No. No more, Tony. I can't stand it." There was a touch of tears in her voice, but she was too new to this, too unskilled to rationalize an ending that she'd never before experienced. Tony kissed her softly on her parted lips, then whispered, "Trust me now, okay?"

When she felt Tony's cheek, now smooth from his shave, glide over her abdomen, the only thought she had was of finding relief. Every nerve ending in her body felt taut, tingling. There was no room for modesty, for shyness.

His hands curved around her knees and she willingly allowed him to part her thighs wide, leaving her totally exposed to his gaze. She felt his warm, gentle breath, the damp touch of his tongue. And then his mouth closed around her, hot and wet, and his teeth carefully nibbled.

No, she'd never survive this. She arched upward,

again begging, feeling the sensations so keenly she screamed. He tightened his hold on her buttocks, holding her steady, forcing her to submit to his torment.

And then it happened and she was only aware of unbelievable pleasure. Tony encouraged her, controlled her, and when the sensations finally began to ebb, he eased, soothing her until she calmed.

When she opened her eyes—a move requiring considerable effort—Tony was beside her again, his hand idly cupping her breast and a look of profound interest on his face. She blinked at him, not understanding that look, and he said without a single qualm, "You've never had an orgasm before, have you?"

Her only recourse seemed to be to close her eyes again. But Tony laughed and kissed her nose. "Don't hide from me, Olivia. Talk to me."

"We're not supposed to be talking."

"No? Well, don't worry. We'll get on to making love again soon. But answer me first."

Disgruntled by his personal question and his persistence, she said, "It never seemed particularly important before. Besides, I told you my two attempts at this failed."

"Your two attempts with a partner." His voice gentled. "That doesn't mean you couldn't have—"

Her eyes rounded when she realized where this questioning was going, and it seemed imperative to divert his attention. "Aren't you supposed to be...uh, excited right about now?"

His smile proved she hadn't fooled him one bit. But

to answer her question, he lifted her limp hand, kissed the palm, then carried it to his erection, curling her fingers around him. For one brief instant, he held himself still, his eyes closing as her fingers flexed. Then he gave a wry grin. "I'm plenty excited. But I'm also enjoying you most thoroughly."

"You're embarrassing me, is what you're doing." She said it with a severe frown, but he only chuckled.

"Why? Because I'm feeling like the most accomplished lover around? You screamed, Olivia." He cupped her cheek and turned her face toward him. "Look at me, honey."

There was that endearment again. She opened her eyes and stared at him. The tenderness in his gaze nearly undid her.

"I'm glad I could give you something you'd never had before. It makes this all seem very...special."

"Tony." She rolled toward him, wanting him again, right now, unwilling to wait another instant.

And then the doorbell rang, and she knew she might not have any choice.

Tony seemed inclined to ignore it at first, but the insistent pounding that came next had him cursing and rising from the bed. As he pulled on jeans, he surveyed her sprawled form, then cursed again. "Don't move. I'll be right back."

Olivia waited until he'd stomped out of the room before scrambling off the bed and wrapping the sheet around herself. She went to the door and opened it a peek, then crept down the hall enough to see who had come calling so early. Tony's brother, John, stood in the entryway, the baby in his arms, and a very worried expression on his face.

Though they spoke in hushed tones, Olivia was able to hear every word.

"I know this is the worst possible time, Tony..."

"You have no idea."

"Yes I do. I saw the car. I assume Olivia is here?"

Tony crossed his arms over his bare chest and said, "What do you want, John?"

"I'm sorry, I really am. And I swear I wouldn't be here if there was anyone else. But Mom and Kate went on a shopping spree this morning and won't be back for hours, and I have to take Lisa to the hospital. You know she wasn't feeling great yesterday is why we left early. And she's always so busy with the three kids, she stays exhausted. But she started running a high fever early last night, coughing and having a hard time breathing, and she's gotten sicker by the hour. I've never seen her like this." There was an edge of desperation in John's tone when he added, "I can't watch my three hellions in a hospital and be with her, too."

Tony immediately straightened, then took the baby from his arms. "Is Lisa going to be okay?"

John looked almost sick himself. "I don't know what's wrong with her, hopefully just the flu, but..."

"Don't give it another thought. Of course I'll take the kids. Where are the other two?"

"Waiting in the car with their mother. I didn't want to leave Lisa alone, and I wasn't certain if you were home." He leaned out the door and waved his hand to get the kids to come in. "I really appreciate this, Tony. I know you probably wish we'd all go..."

"Don't be stupid, John. Just take care of Lisa and keep me informed, okay?"

As John stepped out to gather up a packed diaper bag and some essentials for the other kids, Tony rushed around the corner into the hallway and almost ran into Olivia. He had the overnight bag she'd brought in his left hand while he held the baby in the crook of his right arm. He didn't question her snooping, only led the way into the bedroom. "You heard?"

Olivia could sense the worry in his tone and expression, and was reminded once again how close he was to his family. "Yes. What can I do to help?"

He shook his head. "I'm sorry, babe. Here, can you get dressed real quick?" He no sooner handed her the bag than he was rushing to the living room again to relieve John of the children and send him on his way. Olivia closed the door and sighed. It seemed Tony was going to throw her out, which made sense considering he didn't want her around his family. But it still hurt. While they'd been making love, she'd entirely forgotten everything else in the world, including their twice-damned deal and all the reasons she couldn't feel what she was presently feeling.

Despite all her reasons for needing to stay detached from him, she wanted to stay and help; she wanted to stay, period. Very much.

Her body was still tingling, her heart still racing

from Tony's sensual torment, but she managed to get her slacks and sweater on before he reopened the door. The baby was still nestled in his bare muscled arm, but that didn't stop him from coming toward her, then pulling her close with his free arm. "Damn, I can't believe my luck."

"Things do seem to be conspiring against us."

He brushed a kiss over her lips, then surprised her by asking, "Can you stay?"

Olivia blinked, not certain what to say.

"I know our plans have changed, hell, we might even have the kids all night. But... I don't feel right about all this. It worries me, Lisa coming down sick like that."

Olivia cupped his cheek, touched by his concern, and warmed by the way he'd included her. "You don't want to be alone?"

His jaw tightened and his eyes searched her face. He seemed reluctant to admit it even to himself, but then he nodded. "I guess that's about it."

"We're friends, Tony. Despite any other agreements, I'd like to believe that. And friends help friends. You don't have to worry that I'll read more into this than exists."

He stubbornly ignored her references to their situation, and asked, "Does that mean you'll stay, Olivia? Please?"

At that moment, she would have done anything for him, but of course, she couldn't tell him that. She looked up at him and smiled. "Yes, I'll stay. For as long as you need me."

5

A LOOK OF RELIEF washed over Tony's features, then he hugged her close again. "I believe the coffee is still in the pot. It might be a little strong now, but I could sure use a cup. And the kids are probably hungry. Kids are always hungry, right? So what do you say? You up to breakfast?"

At just that moment, two faces peeked around the door frame, and they were both very solemn. Olivia's heart swelled with emotion for these two small people who were obviously concerned about their mother. She forgot Tony for the moment, forgot that she didn't know anything about kids, and went down on her knees to meet the children at their level.

"Hello. Remember me?"

Six-year-old Luke stared at her with serious eyes, all the energy of yesterday conspicuously missing. "Sure we remember. It was just last night. You was kissing Uncle Tony in his garage."

Olivia felt her face turn pink, but she smiled. "Actually it was the other way around. Your uncle was kissing me."

Maggie, who at three seemed very small and delicate, popped her thumb from her mouth to say with great wisdom, "Uncle Tony likes kissin'. He kisses me lots, too."

And just that easily, Olivia found a rapport. She reached out and tugged Maggie closer, and the little girl came willingly, wrapping one arm around Olivia's neck while holding tight to a tattered blanket with the other. Olivia perched the little girl on her knee. "Are you two hungry? I think your uncle was planning on making breakfast for us."

Maggie nodded, but Luke turned away. Tony stopped him with only a word. "Your mom will be fine, Luke, I promise."

"Dad looked awful scared."

Tony caught Olivia's arm and helped her to stand, then began steering them all toward the kitchen. "Not scared. Upset. There's a big difference. Your dad can't stand to see any of you sick or feeling bad. The fact that your mom is sick makes him feel almost as bad as she does. He wants to take care of all of you, just as your mom does. But he needs time alone with her now, so he can make certain the doctors don't flirt with her too much. He can't watch her if he's busy watching you two."

Luke didn't look as if he understood Tony's humor. "Mom is awful pretty."

"Yes, she is. And so you guys get to stay here with me."

"For how long?"

Tony stopped to stare at Luke, pretending a great affront. "Good grief, boy, you'll have Olivia thinking you don't like me."

Maggie twisted loose from Olivia's hold to say in a very firm voice, "We do so like Unca' Tony. We like him lots." And Olivia couldn't help but smile.

The chatter continued all the while Tony cooked, and with each second, Olivia became more enamored of Tony's familial commitments. The kids, despite their concern, were happy and comfortable to be with him. There was so much love in the air, she could fill her lungs with it. And Tony proved to be as adept at holding a child while cooking as any mother. Olivia wondered if he did so because he enjoyed holding the baby so much, or because he didn't want Olivia to hold him.

Unfortunately, as the day wore on, the latter proved to be true. Not once, even at the most hectic times, did Tony request her assistance with the baby. Not long after they'd finished breakfast John called to say Lisa had pneumonia and they'd be keeping her overnight. She was worn down from all the daily running she did, not to mention having given birth not that long before. And since she was staying at the hospital, John wanted to leave the kids with Tony so he could be free to stay with her.

Tony agreed, and surprisingly, once the kids were assured their mother would be fine and probably home the next day, they seemed thrilled by the idea of staying. Tony promised to bring in a tent that they could set up in front of the fireplace. Maggie asked, "Will Livvy get to sleep with us, too?"

It seemed Tony was caught speechless for a moment, then he said, "If she wants to. And it's Olivia, sweetheart, not Livvy."

"I don't mind, Tony. Actually it's a familiar nickname."

"You look kinda' funny, Olivia." Luke watched her closely, and Olivia was amazed by the child's perception.

"I'm fine, Luke, honest." But hearing little Maggie call her by the same name her own mother and father had always used dredged up long forgotten feelings and left her shaken. And Tony seemed to notice. He held her hand and gave it a squeeze, then went to call his mother and sister to let them know what was going on. He hadn't wanted to tell them Lisa was sick until he knew for certain she'd be all right. Olivia gathered by the one-sided conversation that his mother offered to come and take the children, but Tony only thanked her. He said they had already made plans, and she could have them in the morning, but not before their "camp-out."

Finally, right after an early dinner, Luke and Maggie got bundled up from head to toe and went out back to play. Being children, they seemed impervious to the cold, but Tony insisted that it could only be for a short spell.

Even though the yard was isolated, with no other neighbors in sight, Tony still admonished both children to stay very close by. They could use the tire swing in the tree or play in the small playhouse he and

John had built the preceding summer for just such visits. The infant, Shawn, lay sleeping on a blanket on the floor and Tony and Olivia were left relatively alone.

Tony dropped down beside her on the couch, then grinned. "Man, am I worn-out. Kids, in the plural, can really keep you hopping, can't they?"

She knew he had loved every single minute, that he wasn't really complaining. It had been there on his face, the way he smiled, the way he held the baby and teased Maggie and spoke to Luke.

She licked her lips nervously and slanted him a cautious look. "I would have been glad to help you out a little, you know." She said it tentatively, hoping to broach the topic without setting off any alarm bells.

But all he did was pat her thigh in a now familiar way. "You help a lot just by being here. Pneumonia. Can you imagine that? Lisa always seems so healthy. But John said the doctor told him it could bring you low in just a few hours."

"Will she have to stay in the hospital long?"

"No. She'll probably get to come home tomorrow. And Mom and Kate are already making plans to take turns helping her out until she's completely well again. John is swearing he's going to hire someone to come and clean for her from now on, but he said Lisa told him to forget it. She's funny about her house, likes to do things a certain way, you know?"

His statement didn't really require an answer, and Olivia couldn't have given him one anyway. "Your whole family really sticks together, don't they?"

He seemed surprised by her question. "Of course we do."

"I mean, even though Lisa isn't really part of your family..."

"She's married to John. She's the mother of my niece and nephews. She's part of the family."

And that was that, Olivia supposed. It would be so nice to belong to such a family. She said without thinking, "When Maggie called me Livvy... It, well, it reminded me of when I was a child. That was what my mother and father always called me. But I'd forgotten until she said it."

Tony wrapped one large hand around the back of her neck and tugged her closer. His lips touched her temple, and she could feel their movement against her skin as he spoke. "I figured it must have been something like that. I'm sorry, Olivia. You looked so damn sad."

"No. Not sad really." She tried her best to look cavalier over the subject, even so far as giving him a smile. "It's been so long, I've forgotten what it's like to miss them. I guess I'm used to being alone."

It was a horrible lie, because who could actually get accustomed to spending her life alone? There was never anyone to share the triumphs, which made them seem almost hollow, and when the struggles to get ahead occasionally became too much, she had only herself to lean on.

Tony was staring at her in his intent, probing way and Olivia had the horrible suspicion he was reading her thoughts, knowing exactly what it was she concealed, and how empty she often felt.

He looked down at her hands, which were tightly pressed together in her lap, then covered them with one of his own. "Is that why you've isolated yourself?"

"I haven't."

His gaze snapped back to her face, as if struck that she would deny such an obvious thing. "Of course you have. You keep to yourself, don't date, don't form long-standing friendships. You put everything you have into the lingerie shops. It's almost like you're afraid of getting involved."

"I am not afraid." She didn't know what else she could say. She felt defensive, as if she had to explain her choice of life-style, but that was impossible. She would never be able to give Tony the truth.

"It's not natural for a woman like you to still be single, to not want some kind of commitment."

Despite herself, she stiffened. "A woman like me? What exactly is that supposed to mean?"

Tony closed his eyes and made a sound of frustration. "I'm sorry. I didn't mean that the way it sounded. It's just that...I never thought of you as you are. You always seemed pleasant enough, but so businesslike and...well, detached. And here you are, a very warm, caring woman, wearing sexy lingerie that makes me go a little crazy and looking so damn sweet and vulnerable at the most surprising times."

"Tony..." She didn't like being labeled vulnerable any more than she liked feeling defensive.

"I don't understand you, Olivia, and I want to. I really do."

"But why?"

He quirked a smile. "Don't sound so panicked. I promise, I'm not asking for orange blossoms and golden rings. I just...I guess I like you more than I thought I would."

"Sex has a way of making a man feel like that. Believe me, it will pass."

He reached out to wrap a lock of her hair around his finger, then gently pulled until her face was closer to his. His tone was low, his expression heated. "Honey, you don't know enough about men and sex to make that assumption." He laid his palm warmly on her thigh, gently squeezing. "And I'd say that nasty little comment deserves some form of retribution, wouldn't you?"

Olivia tried to pull away, but she couldn't get very far. She wasn't afraid of Tony, but she didn't trust the look in his eyes. He was pushing, and there was too much she could never tell him.

"I didn't mean it to sound nasty, exactly." She was beginning to feel cornered, and that made her so very nervous. Then she went on the attack, hoping to force him to back off. "Dammit, Tony, we agreed not to get personal, right? And this discussion is getting very personal. You want a baby from me, not my life history. Why don't we talk about sex instead?" Trying to be subtle, she leaned into him, allowing her breasts to brush against his chest.

He allowed her closeness, but his expression didn't change. "Since I do want a baby from you, and you don't appear to be the woman I first thought you to be, I think your family history is very relevant." He continued to maintain his gentle hold on her hair as his hand left her thigh and curved around her waist.

She drew in a sharp breath when his fingers slipped upward to tease against the outer curves of her breast. She tried to squirm, to get his hand exactly where she wanted it, but he only grinned and continued to tease.

It was enough to set off her temper, and without thinking she jerked upright again. But Tony only pulled her back, using her hair as a leash.

Olivia gritted her teeth. "I'm not going to sit and let you practice your intimidation tactics. This isn't a boardroom."

"No, and it's not the bedroom, either. So stop trying to distract me with sex—believe me, we'll get back to that as soon as possible. Just tell me a little about your folks." He was still speaking in that soft, determined tone, and she could feel his stubbornness. The man had it in buckets.

It was apparent he wasn't going to give up, so she did. She just wasn't practiced enough to play this kind of game with a man. "Never say I don't know when to restructure my plans."

"And your plans were to run the show?"

"Something like that. But it's not important now."

Tony laughed softly, then turned her head toward him so he could kiss her mouth. His quick, soft peck turned into a lingering kiss, and he gave a low curse when he finally managed to pull himself away. "You're a fast learner, but I'm afraid I'm too curious to let you get away with it. Go ahead now. Tell me about your parents."

Her sigh was long, indicating her reluctance. "They were poor, not overly educated, and they worked harder than anybody I know." Speaking of them brought a tightness to her chest that always wanted to linger. She tried clearing her throat, but the discomfort remained. "Our furniture was usually tattered, but it was always clean. My mother kept an immaculate house."

"You were close with them?"

She simply couldn't remember—and it pained her. There were too many other memories in the way of the good times. "We didn't have much daily time to do things together. Whenever possible, my mother would make me a special cake, and my dad always kissed me good-night, no matter how late he got in. But they weren't always happy, which I suppose makes sense seeing how poor we were."

She drew a deep breath, the tightness now nearly choking her, and before she knew she would say the words, they tumbled out. "My parents loved me, they really did, and they tried to do the best for me that they could, but...sometimes they made mistakes."

Easing closer, Tony twined his fingers through her hair and began massaging her scalp. His nearness touched her, made some of the hurt from the memories fade.

He leaned down and placed a kiss on the bridge of her nose. "All parents make mistakes, honey. It's a built-in factor that you can't be a perfect parent."

Olivia only nodded, since she had no idea how other parents did things. But he had questions, and she wanted to give him his answers quickly, to get the telling over with so she could forget it all again. "I was an only child and we lived on the riverbank in a tiny little nothing town called Hattsburg, Mississippi. My mother worked at the local market, my father at the one factory in town. Sometimes...sometimes he drank too much. It was the way he escaped, my mom used to say."

Tony leaned into her, giving her silent comfort. She drew a deep breath and rushed through the rest of the story. "They died on the river, using a boat that couldn't have passed safety standards on its best day, but was especially hazardous in bad weather. The river had swelled from spring rains, and the boat capsized. My father was drunk and didn't use good judgment, the deputy said. He was knocked out when he went overboard and died before they reached the hospital. My mother had tried to save him, but the water was still frigid, and she suffered exposure and multiple injuries. And grief. She died in the hospital not too many days after my father."

She drew a deep breath, knowing the unwanted feelings would crowd her if she let them. She shook her head at herself, denying the feelings, the hurt. "I don't really miss them anymore, because I can hardly remember ever having a family. You're really pretty lucky, you know."

He was silent over that, and Olivia wondered if she'd said too much, if he was again having second thoughts about allowing her around his family. But then he tipped her chin up and without a word began nibbling lightly on her lips. She exchanged one set of concerns for another. "Tony... Don't tease me anymore. I swear, I don't think I can take it and there's no way we can do anything about it now."

"No, we can't. But I just like touching you. Don't deny me that." He slipped his tongue into her mouth, holding her head steady with his hand still on the back of her neck.

"When..." She gasped as his head lifted and his hand covered her breast, then she started over. "When will we be able to try again?"

"My mother will pick the kids up in the morning. Do you have to be at work early?"

His fingers found her nipple, encouraging her to give the right answer. After a breathless moan, she said, "I can take the morning off."

"Good. I have to go in for a while in the afternoon, but I want you to go with me. There's something I want to show you."

Olivia would have questioned that, but he suddenly tunneled both hands into her hair and leaned her into the padded back of the couch, his mouth ravenous, moving over her face, her throat.

"God, I think I've been wanting you forever."

Olivia thrilled at the words. It was such a pleasant alternative, going from the distressing memories of her childhood to the newfound feelings of adult desire, her mind simply accepted the change with no lingering remorse. Then a small, outraged voice intruded, and she practically leapt off the couch.

"Sheeesh! You guys are gross."

Luke stood there, his hands on his narrow hips, his skinny legs braced wide apart and a look of total disgust on his face.

With a sigh that turned into a laugh, Tony asked, "What do you want, squirt?"

"I wanted you to come out and toss with me. Maggie can't catch nothin'."

Tony considered it a moment, but his gaze kept going to the baby. She could tell the idea of a game of catch was enticing for him, and yet he was going to refuse. Olivia rolled her eyes. "Go on, Tony. If the baby starts fussing, I'll come get you."

Cupping her cheek, Tony drifted his thumb over her lips and whispered, "I don't want to leave you alone."

Again, Luke complained. "You two are worse than Mom and Dad!"

Olivia couldn't help but laugh. "Will you go on, before Luke gets sick? He's starting to turn a funny shade of green."

That had Luke laughing and looking for a mirror so he could see for himself.

Olivia pushed at Tony's solid shoulders. "Go on. I'll be fine. I'll just watch a little television."

"You're sure?"

"I'm positive. Now go."

It was a cool November day, and Tony pulled on his down jacket before stepping out the back door. Olivia went to the window to watch. The kids laughed and tackled Tony as he tried to throw the ball, and they all three went down in a pile. Tony began tickling Luke, while at the same time he managed to toss Maggie in the air. Olivia felt something damp on her cheek, and when she went to brush it away, she realized it was a tear.

Why the sight of Tony's gorgeous, healthy body in play with two kids should make her cry, she didn't know. It wasn't as if he wouldn't eventually get the child he wanted—and obviously deserved. He'd make a remarkable father, and she envied him the opportunity to be a parent. But she wasn't actually hampering him, only slowing him down for a few weeks. And what was that when compared with a lifetime of having a child of your own?

She would have stood there watching them forever, but the baby started to fuss, and since Olivia assumed he couldn't be hungry, not after Tony had just given him a bottle before putting him down, she decided he might just want to be held.

She knew she did.

Being very careful, she lifted the baby in her arms, and like a small turtle, he stretched his head up to look at her. She grinned at his pouting expression. It was almost as if he were disgruntled at waking to unfamiliar surroundings. She cuddled him close and patted his back and listened to his lusty little yawn.

Sitting in the large padded chair not far from where little Shawn had been sleeping, she settled them both there. It was easy to relax while inhaling his unique, sweet baby scent. And Shawn seemed to like her, resting against her in a posture of trust, with his little head against her breasts, his legs tucked up against her belly. By instinct alone, she hummed a melody she knew and gently swayed in the chair, lulling him. Before long, she was yawning as well, and thinking that if she could never have a baby of her own, at least now she'd know what it was like to hold one.

TONY CAME IN CARRYING Maggie and listening to Luke tell him all the things he wanted for Christmas. It was an impressive list, and he was thinking Luke might be just a bit spoiled, then decided he'd buy him the expensive remote-control car he wanted. Grinning, he knew John would have a fit, but it didn't matter. That's what uncles were for—to indulge their nephews.

He stopped cold when he walked into the family room and found Olivia curled up in a chair with Shawn sleeping in her arms. Immediately he hushed Luke and Maggie, not wanting Olivia to awaken. In fact, he could have stood there for hours just looking at her.

It was such a revelation, discovering her like this and having his heart suddenly acknowledge all the things it had been denying. It seemed as if all his strength had just been stripped away, leaving him raw and unsteady.

This was what he wanted.

He wanted to come in from playing with the kids— his kids—and find his woman resting with his baby in her arms. He wanted to coddle her, to love her. He wanted an entire family to look after, not just a single baby. He wanted to share all his love, and have it returned. He wanted it all.

With his heart thundering and his stomach tight, he set little Maggie down and pulled Luke close. Speaking in hushed tones, he told the children, "I want you to get the bag your dad brought and find your pajamas, then go into the bathroom and wash up."

"Carry me." Maggie reached up again, but Tony shook his head.

"Not this time, munchkin. Luke, can you help Maggie with her clothes?"

"Sure. She sometimes puts her stuff on backwards."

Maggie frowned. "I'm only a little girl, so it's okay. Mommy says so."

Tony grinned. "And your mom is right." He gave Maggie a quick squeeze. "You can leave your clothes in the bathroom and I'll pick them up in a bit. Get ready for bed and I'll get the tent set up, okay?"

Luke sidled close to get his own hug. "Can we have marshmallows and chocolate?"

"I think I have some cocoa left. We'll check when you've finished up. Put your toothbrushes in the bathroom, though, so we don't forget to brush before we go to bed."

"It's not bedtime yet."

Tony patted Luke's head, hearing the touch of anxiety there. "Nope. We still have to read a story, too. But when it is time, I promise to sleep close by you, okay?"

Trying not to look too relieved, Luke nodded. "Maggie'll like that."

"Carry me."

Again Maggie lifted her arms to Tony, and he almost gave in. Then he shook his head. "Go on, imp. Luke will give you a hand."

She didn't look happy about it, but she let Luke take her hand and lead her down the hall. Tony felt a swell of pride at what good kids they were. He hoped, when Olivia finally conceived, that he'd be half as a good a parent as his brother John was.

That thought had his stomach roiling again, and he went back in to look at Olivia. She hadn't moved a single muscle. He'd never thought it before, but looking at her now, relaxed with a small, content smile on her face, she was a very beautiful woman. He swallowed the lump of emotion in his throat, then carefully crept toward her chair.

She was obviously exhausted, the past two days wearing on her. He knew he'd slept little, and she'd confessed to the same problem. What they were doing, what they planned, it was enough to rattle a person's thoughts.

Seeing her in sleep, though, with all her pride and stubbornness and the attitude she generally affected wiped away by total relaxation, proved to be a great insight. He'd always seen Olivia in one way, as if any woman could be one-dimensional. He should have known Olivia would be more complex than most.

Talking about her family had upset her, had left her struggling for words in a way he'd never witnessed before. Her pain had become his, and he'd found himself wanting only to distract her, to ease her. When he'd kissed her, it had been with the intent to console, but as always with Olivia since starting this strange bit of business, one touch had left him wanting another, and for a brief moment, he'd actually forgotten Maggie and Luke outside.

It was a good thing Luke had walked in when he did, because Tony didn't want her thinking everything between them was about sex, or even about getting a baby. As she'd told him earlier, they were friends. Certainly they were closer friends now than he'd ever envisioned them being, but he liked it, and he sensed a need in her to be reassured. He planned to do just that.

Little Shawn wiggled, then snuggled into her breast, and without opening her eyes, Olivia gently patted his back and made soft *shushing* sounds. Tony reached out and laid his hand over hers, hoping to convey so much with that one small gesture.

Olivia's eyes snapped open, but she didn't move or jar the baby in any way. It took her a moment to re-orient herself, then she smiled. "Hi."

That one whispered word had his chest squeezing again. "Hi."

"He wanted to be held."

Her voice, pitched low and husky from sleep, rubbed over him like a caress. "So I see."

"He sleeps a lot, doesn't he?"

"He's still considered a newborn. I suppose," he whispered, staring into her dark eyes and wanting so much to hold her, "we should get a book on babies, one that tells you what to expect so we'll be prepared when ours is born."

A look of such intense pain filled her eyes he reached for her without thinking. "What is it, Olivia? Are you okay?"

She swallowed twice, then took a deep breath. "I'm okay. It's just...Tony, will you be very disappointed if I don't conceive? I mean, what if we try the agreed two weeks, and it just doesn't happen?"

"We'll keep trying." He was positive. He didn't want any other woman to birth his child. He wanted this woman.

"I...I don't know if that's a good idea. We agreed—"

He bridged his arms around her hips and laid his head against her thighs. Her hand touched his nape, then she threaded her fingers through his hair. "Tony?"

"Shh. You're borrowing trouble. Let's just wait and

see what happens." He continued to hold her like that until he heard the kids start out of the bathroom. With a sigh, he sat up. "I guess I'd better get started on that tent. Will you camp out with us tonight?"

She shook her head. "I shouldn't. I didn't bring any pajamas or my toothbrush or any—"

"I have a silly pair of Mickey Mouse pajamas Kate bought for me one year as a joke. You can use those. And I have an extra toothbrush."

"You do? Should I ask why?"

Grinning, he came to his feet. "I'd rather you didn't."

Olivia frowned at him, and he decided he liked her small show of jealousy, even if he knew she would deny suffering such an emotion.

Being careful not to wake him, he lifted Shawn and returned him to his blanket. "Come on. You can help me pitch a tent."

Her frown left, and to his relief, she joined in whole-heartedly. It took them a half hour to get the tent assembled. They shoved all the furniture back so the tent sat in the middle of the room. Olivia lit a fire in the fireplace while Tony searched through his kitchen for marshmallows and cocoa. Shawn woke up and began fussing, and though Olivia wanted to help, she was hopeless at changing a diaper. Tony laughed at her efforts, then showed her the proper way to do it. Her intent fascination through the routine process had him grinning long after the job was done.

He knew she wanted to give Shawn his bottle, but

she held back, pretending a great interest in the silly, rather long-winded story Maggie was telling her about a cartoon character on her favorite preschool show. Tony watched her surreptitiously, and a plan began to form.

Maybe, because of all she'd been through as a child, Olivia only thought she didn't want a family. Maybe he could convince her otherwise. As soon as the idea hit, he felt a sick sort of trepidation. Like any man, the thought of rejection was repugnant to him. And he knew he was being overly emotional about the whole thing, but this particular situation was one to inspire romantic notions. Being alone with a woman, acting as a family to three children, left his need for his own family with a sharpened edge.

But his original plan was much more realistic, and much easier to plan around. He *knew* he could love a child, that he could be a good father. He had the example of his own father, not to mention his brother and brother-in-law to go by. But a wife...that was a chancy matter. Could he really count on Olivia to restructure her life to fit a family into her busy schedule?

He decided what he needed was more time—time to watch her with the children, to be with her. He'd take her to the office tomorrow and show her the expansion plans beginning with the new Northwestern Crown. He'd planned to do that anyway, to judge her reaction to the site for her new lingerie shop.

In the meantime...

He went over to her, not really giving her a choice,

and put Shawn in her lap. She opened her dark eyes wide and stared at him, looking hopeful, and a bit unsure of herself. Then he handed her the bottle of formula, and watched as Shawn began to fuss, and Olivia looked from him to the baby and back again.

"I think he's hungry, honey. Would you mind?"

"You want me to feed him?"

"Just keep the bottle up so he doesn't suck air, and keep a napkin under his chin because he tends to make a mess of it."

Looking as if she'd just been handed the world, Olivia carefully situated bottle and baby, then managed to listen as Maggie picked up where she'd been interrupted.

His heart seemed to swell, watching Olivia struggle with the baby. And more and more, he found himself wondering if keeping only the baby wouldn't mean giving up the better half of the deal.

6

AFTER SEVERAL STORIES and whispered giggles, Maggie and Luke finally fell asleep. It was way past their usual bedtime, but it had proven very difficult to get the kids to settle down. The combination of worrying about their mother, being in different surroundings and their general excitement, had all conspired to keep them wide-awake.

Tony had arranged everyone in a row, with Luke first, then himself, then Maggie, then Olivia. He would have preferred to have her right next to him, but he didn't trust himself, and he wasn't into self-torture. Now, at nearly midnight, Tony turned his head to look at Olivia, and even in the dim interior of the tent, he could see that her eyes were open. He reached across Maggie, who was taking up more room than one little three-year-old girl should, and slid one finger down Olivia's arm. Her eyes slanted in his direction, and she smiled. "They're asleep?"

He answered in the same hushed tone. "I do believe so."

"I've never slept on the floor before."

He grinned, then tugged on the sleeve of the pajamas she wore until she gave him her hand. "A lot of new experiences today, huh?"

When she bit her lip, he suppressed a laugh and said, "I was talking about wearing Micky Mouse pajamas. And giving a baby a bottle. And camping out in the family room with a three-year-old snoring next to you."

Olivia flashed her own grin. "And here I thought you meant something entirely different."

"Are you enjoying yourself?"

Turning on her side to face him, she laced her fingers with his, and they allowed their arms to rest over Maggie. The little girl sighed in her sleep. "You know, I believe I am having fun. I'd always thought of you as a stuffy businessman, and here you are, an adventurer."

"Me, stuffy? You're the one who eats, drinks and sleeps business."

She gave him another cheeky grin. "I learned from you."

"Ah, so it's my fault you're so ruthless?" His grin belied any insult.

"I'm serious. I've always respected you very much. Everyone does. When I negotiated my first shop in your hotels, I'd already read everything I could find on you. And there was plenty. You're considered a golden boy, you know. You took a mediocre hotel chain and turned it around to one of the fastest growing, most recognizable names in the industry. You gave new meaning to the name Austin Crown."

It was unbelievable the amount of pride he felt hearing her sing his praises. Of course he'd heard it before, but it meant more coming from Olivia. And he decided he liked this, liked talking quietly in the dark, getting to know her better, letting her know him. He seldom volunteered information about himself, but now, it seemed the most natural thing in the world.

"When my father died, I knew I had to do something to distract myself. It wasn't an easy time, and he'd been a really fantastic father—the best. He'd taught me what I needed to know in the industry, but like John, he refused to neglect his family to devote the time necessary to make the business what it is today. Sometimes I wonder if he'd lived, exactly where I'd be right now."

She answered with absolute conviction. "You'd have had your own business. You're a very driven, success-oriented man. I'll bet you were an overachiever in school, too, weren't you?"

He laughed quietly, knowing she'd pegged him. "I suppose. And it's not that I regret the life I've led. But there could have been so much more." He knew she understood when she squeezed his hand.

"And there will be. Now. You'll have your own family, Tony, just wait. You've still got plenty of time to do anything you want to do. You're young and intelligent and very handsome, and—"

It disturbed him, having her talk about his life with her being no part of it. Though that had been his original plan, and could still work out to be the best solution, he instinctively balked at the thought of losing her. Interrupting her to halt the words, he teased, "Very handsome, hmm?"

"Quit fishing for compliments. You know what you look like. Why not be honest about it?"

The glow from the fireplace barely penetrated the thick canvas of the tent, leaving the outline of Olivia's body a mere shadow beneath her blanket. But her eyes, so wide and sweet, were as discernible as her slight smile. "That's one of the things I like about you, Olivia. You believe in honesty. You're outspoken and truthful to a fault. I don't have to guess at your motives."

He felt her sudden stillness, the way she seemed to withdraw emotionally. She didn't say anything, though the tension was thick, and then she was trying to pull away. "We better get some sleep. As I told you, I didn't rest much last night."

He didn't understand the way her mood had abruptly altered, but he decided he wouldn't allow her to pull completely away from him. Rather than question her when she seemed so anxious, he merely replied to her statement. Holding tight to her fingers, he whispered, "I'm sorry you're tired, but I'm glad I didn't suffer alone." She had nothing to say to that, so he added, "Good night, sweetheart. If you need anything during the night, let me know."

Pillowing her head on her arm, she closed her eyes and very deliberately shut him out.

But she didn't take her hand away. And then he heard her whisper, "Good night, Tony."

IT WAS VERY EARLY when Olivia felt a puff of moist breath against her cheek. She opened one eye and jerked in startled surprise before she recognized the faint outline of Maggie's face in the dim interior of the tent. "What is it?"

Maggie's nose touched her cheek and she realized the child was trying to see her clearly. "Livvy, I gotta pee."

"Oh." For a second, Olivia drew a blank. She glanced at Tony to see that Luke was practically lying on top of him, draped sideways over his chest. They'd put Shawn to sleep outside the tent, surrounded by the cushions off the couch so no one would accidentally get up in the night and step on him. Twice, she had heard him fuss, but both times Tony had quietly slipped from the tent to prepare the baby's bottle.

Olivia didn't want to wake him again for something so minor, but she honestly had no idea how to deal with Maggie's request. "Do you, uh...know how to go to the potty by yourself?"

She could barely see the bobbing of Maggie's head. "But you come wif me."

"Oh." Olivia was beginning to feel like an idiot. Of course the little girl wouldn't want to go on her own. The house was dark and unfamiliar. "Okay. But let's be quiet so we don't wake anyone up."

They crawled out of the tent, and Maggie caught at the hem of the Micky Mouse pajama top, then held her arms in the air. "Carry me."

Since Maggie wasn't really asking, but insisting,

Olivia lifted her sturdy little body and groped her way down the hall. The fluorescent bathroom light was bright and made them both squint. Olivia watched Maggie struggle with her nightgown, then she asked, "Do you...um, need any help?"

Shaking her head, Maggie said, "Stay wif me."

"Right. I won't go anywhere."

Maggie grinned at her, and Olivia felt rather complimented that her company had been required for such a female outing. Hadn't she seen plenty of women visit the "ladies' room" in groups? It was practically a tradition, and Maggie had just given her a part of it. She leaned against the wall and waited, and when Maggie had finished and again said, "Carry me," Olivia didn't hesitate. In fact, she found she liked having the small warm body clinging to her, trusting her.

They entered the tent without making a sound, but no sooner had she settled Maggie than she heard Tony say, "You have all the natural instincts, Olivia."

This time, the reference to something that could never be didn't bother her. In fact, she felt a reluctant grin and realized she felt good. Damn good. "Go to sleep, Tony."

"Yeah," Maggie said. "Go sleep, Tony." And within seconds, the tent was again filled with soft snoring.

TONY'S MOTHER SHOWED UP at eight-thirty with a bag of doughnuts and the news that Lisa was feeling much improved, except for a great deal of lingering exhaustion. The penicillin had done its magic and she was more than anxious to see her children again.

"I'm going to take them to the hospital to visit her this morning," Sue said, "and they're hopeful she can come home this afternoon, after the doctor makes his rounds and checks her over."

"Isn't that rushing it a bit?" Tony asked. They were sitting at the dining-room table while Maggie and Luke gobbled doughnuts in the kitchen. Sue held Shawn, and every so often she'd make faces at him and babble in baby talk or nibble on his ears or feet. Tony glanced at Olivia and saw she was fascinated by his mother's behavior. In his family, no one felt the least hesitation in playing with a child—and acting like a fool in the process.

"She seemed to be doing okay to me, but of course, I'm not a doctor." Sue smiled at Olivia. "You know how it is with mothers. They can't bear to be away from their kids. Why, if they try to keep her another day while she's complaining and begging to leave, she's liable to make herself sick with worry. She's afraid the kids are terrorizing Tony. Of course, she didn't know he had you here to help him."

The sound of suggestion in his mother's tone couldn't have been missed by a deaf man. Tony glanced at Olivia again, but she was only smiling. He felt...proud, dammit. Proud of the way Olivia had greeted his mother, her natural grace and composure. Being caught in your lover's house by your lover's mother wasn't something Olivia was used to. But she'd handled the situation remarkably well.

Dressed in casual khaki slacks with a sharp pleat and a black pullover sweater, she didn't look like a woman who had spent the night on the floor. She'd been up and dressed when he opened his eyes, and that had annoyed him. Usually the idea of facing a woman in the morning was an unpleasant prospect, but with Olivia, he'd wanted to see her sleeping in his house. He'd wanted to make her coffee and awaken her with a kiss. Instead she was the one who had prepared the coffee, and all traces of peaceful rest had been washed from her big brown eyes before he'd even crawled from the tent. She was again the composed, elegant lady he'd come to know through business, and while he appreciated the picture she made, he wanted to see that softer, more accessible side of her more often.

Olivia laughed at his mother's comments, and Tony could only stare, wanting her again. Always wanting her. The woman didn't have to do more than walk toward him and he got hard.

"Tony did all the work, Sue. I'm afraid I haven't had much experience with children. But please, tell Lisa that the kids were adorable. I very much enjoyed myself."

It was at that moment Maggie appeared at Olivia's side. Her face and hands were sticky with doughnut glaze, and without missing a beat, Olivia picked up a napkin and began wiping off the worst of it. Maggie grinned and said, "Carry me, Livvy."

Olivia bent down to scoop Maggie into her lap. "And where are we going?"

"Potty."

Turning to Sue, she said, "Excuse me just a moment."

She'd done that so naturally, without any hesitation at all, Tony knew he was making progress. Toward what end, he wasn't certain, but he took great satisfaction from the progress just the same.

He didn't realize he was smiling as he watched her leave the room until his mother nudged him with her foot. "She's a natural."

He laughed. "I told her the same thing last night."

Sue made a big production of rearranging Shawn's blanket. "It's worked out nice that she was here yesterday when John came by."

"I could have managed on my own."

"You've never had all three kids overnight before."

"True. But we'd have muddled through. Actually Shawn was the easiest to look after. He still sleeps most of the day away." It was apparent his small talk hadn't distracted his mother one iota. She had that look about her that gave him pause and let him know she was set on a course.

"So...what was Olivia doing here?"

Never let it be said that his mother couldn't use subtlety when it was required. "Women have been in my house before."

"It's been a while, though. And Olivia, unless I miss my guess, isn't just another woman."

Their relationship was too complicated by far to explain to his mother. Especially since he didn't understand it himself. He decided to nip her curiosity and parental meddling in the bud, at least until he could sort out his own feelings. "Olivia is more into business than I am. She wants to get ahead, not stay at home."

"So? Plenty of women work these days and tend a family, too. And you're not exactly helpless. I think between the two of you..."

"Mom, you're way ahead of yourself. Olivia is very clear on the fact she doesn't want a husband or family. She told me that herself. She would be totally unsuitable as a wife, so stop trying to plot against me."

Sue glanced up at the doorway, then cleared her throat. Olivia stood there, her face pink with embarrassment and a stricken look in her eyes. Tony wanted to curse; he wanted to stand up and hold her close and swear he hadn't meant what he'd just said. But there was his mother to consider, and besides, he didn't know how much of what he'd said might be true.

Olivia took the problem out of his hands by forcing a smile, then retaking her seat. "I'm afraid he's right, Sue. I'm not marriage material. This is the closest I've ever come to playing house, and I'm not at all certain I was successful. Which is okay. I'm a businesswoman, with not a domestic bone in my body." She laughed, but Tony knew her laughs now, and this one wasn't genuine. "I'm not cut out for this sort of thing. But after watching Tony last night, I'm convinced he is. He should have a few children of his own."

His mother agreed, then made deliberate small talk, but the tension in the air refused to dissipate. Once again Olivia was invited for Thanksgiving dinner, but the invitation was left open. And when the children were done eating and had their teeth brushed, Sue bustled them toward the door.

Giving Tony a listen-to-your-mother look, she said, "Try to talk Olivia into coming for Thanksgiving." Then to Olivia, "It's very casual and relaxed. With all the kids, it couldn't be any other way. But now that I know the children don't bother you—"

Maggie spoke up and said, "We don't bother, Livvy. She likes us."

Olivia patted her head and smiled. "Of course I do."

So Luke added, "Then you'll come? Grandma makes lots of desserts."

That was obviously supposed to be enough inducement to tilt the scales. Tony laughed. "I'll see what I can do about persuading her, guys, okay?"

There was another round of hugs, and this time Olivia didn't look nearly so uncomfortable. And when he finally closed the door, Tony turned to her and gave his best wolfish grin. "Now, you."

"Me, what?"

"How did you get up so early today and put yourself together so well without making a sound?"

"Put myself together?"

"Yeah." He reached out to smooth his hand over her tidy hair. She'd pulled it back into a French braid that looked both casual and classic. She wore only the faintest touch of makeup—all that was needed with her dark lashes and brows and perfect complexion. "You sure don't look like a woman who camped on the floor of a tent last night."

"Oh." Olivia reached up and put her hands on his shoulders. With flat heels on, she stood just a few inches shorter than he. "I knew your mother was coming, and I thought it might be less awkward if I was up and about when she arrived."

"These are the clothes you had packed in that bag?"

"Yes. Not dressy, but suitable for just about anything."

Skimming his gaze down her body, he said, "You look wonderful. As always." Then his attention was drawn to her breasts, and he asked with increased interest, "Are you wearing sexy underwear again?"

"No."

"No?" She surprised him. "Why not? I thought you liked wearing that stuff. I was looking forward to you making me crazy again."

She cleared her throat. "I hadn't planned to spend the night. So just as I didn't pack a toothbrush, I didn't pack additional underthings."

"You didn't... Then what are you wearing underneath?"

"Nothing."

He froze for a heartbeat, then groaned and leaned down toward her mouth. "Next time, wake me before you get up."

Again, she surprised him. She pulled away and

wrapped her arms around her stomach. "I don't think there should be a next time. This...spending the night, playing with children, morning visits with your mother—they weren't part of the deal, Tony."

He wanted to touch her, but her stance clearly warned him away. When he bent to try to read her expression, she kept her head averted. "I thought you enjoyed yourself."

Waving a hand to indicate the entire morning and night before, she said, "I wasn't supposed to be enjoying—" she waved her hand again "—all that. I was supposed to be enjoying...well..."

Tony grinned. "Ah. I've neglected my end of the bargain, haven't I? And I did promise to make it up to you."

She jerked away when he reached for her, her brows lowered in a stern frown. "You did not disappoint me! I meant..."

Tony caught her despite her resistance, then gently eased her into his body. With his lips barely touching hers, he said, "You don't even know what you're missing yet."

Again, she tried to protest, but he was done discussing issues he'd rather avoid, so he silenced her in the best way known to man.

And this time, she voiced not a single complaint.

OLIVIA MOANED as the sensations just kept building. Tony was poised over her, in her, and his eyes held hers, touching her as intimately as his body did.

He was right. She hadn't known what she was missing.

One large warm hand curved around her buttocks, then urged her into a rhythm. "Move with me, sweetheart. That's it." He groaned, his eyes briefly closing as he fought for control. She loved that, loved watching him struggle, loved knowing she had such an effect on him.

When he hooked his arms under her legs and lifted them high, leaving her totally open and vulnerable, she nearly panicked. He was so deep that her feelings of pleasure were mixed with fear. Tony bent to press a kiss to her lax mouth.

"Shh. It's all right." He thrust just a little harder, watching her face. "Tell me if I hurt you."

"Tony..."

"Deep, honey, the book said deep. Remember? This was your idea."

She recalled sitting in the restaurant and taunting him about methods devised to better ensure conception. But what she felt now had nothing to do with receiving his sperm and everything to do with pleasure so intense it was frightening.

She felt the pressure build, felt Tony's heat washing over her, his scent filling her lungs, and she squeezed her eyes shut as her climax hit.

"Open your eyes!"

Tony's demand barely penetrated, but she managed to get her lids to lift, and then she connected with him in a way that went beyond the activities of their bodies.

His eyes were bright, his face flushed, and as she watched he groaned, his jaw tight, his gaze locked to hers, and she knew he was experiencing his own explosive orgasm. She felt it with him, and her own again, and then he lowered himself, in slow degrees, to rest completely over her.

It seemed too much to bear, the emotional side to lovemaking, and she wondered that other people didn't find it too overwhelming. Tears came to her eyes, her breath starting to shudder, but thankfully, Tony was unaware, as he still struggled for his own breath. When he started to move away, she tightened her hold.

He wrapped his arms more firmly around her and pressed his face beside hers. "You're something else, you know that?"

She wondered if that was true. Was it always this way, or did they do something special? It certainly seemed special to her.

"What is it, honey?" Tony lifted away and smoothed her hair from her face. He noticed a tear and kissed it from her cheek, then smiled. "I can hear you thinking."

"That's impossible."

"Nope. I really can. You're worrying about something, aren't you?"

She noticed he wasn't apologizing this time for not doing it right. In fact, he looked downright smug, so she assumed this was how it was supposed to be. But...
"It gets more intense every time."

"And that worries you?"

Shrugging her bare shoulders, she looked away from his astute gaze and mumbled, "Is it supposed to be like that?"

She could hear the smile in his tone. "Between us, yes."

"But not with other people?"

"Olivia." She knew she amused him and she frowned. He smoothed his thumb over her brow, making her relax again.

"Sex is different with everyone. It's certainly never been like this for me before, but it's nothing to worry about. Some people can be very cavalier about intimacy, but you're just not that way."

"Are you?"

He hesitated, then kissed her again. "I don't know. To me, sex is natural and not something to be ashamed of. But it was never just casual, either. I had to care for a woman. I didn't indulge in one-night stands. But...it was never quite like this. Not the way it is with you."

This time, Olivia couldn't look away. "Doesn't that bother you?"

His laugh made her jump, coming so unexpectedly. "No. It probably should, but...damn, I like it."

He forestalled all her other questions by rising from the bed, then looking down at her body. Rather than feeling embarrassment, she felt proud that he took pleasure in the sight of her. Then he reached down and smacked his open palm against her hip. "Come on, woman. Duty calls. I need to go into the office."

She stretched, not really wanting to leave his bed but

knowing he was right. "I have to make a few calls, also."

"Will you come to my office with me?"

"Ah, the mysterious thing you have to show me. What is it, Tony?"

"You'll see when we get there."

Olivia rose and headed for the bathroom, amazed at how quickly she was getting used to being naked in front of a man. "I'll have to meet you there. I need to go home and shower properly and change, and check in at the office. I've got to hire a new manager now, you know."

She closed the bathroom door and reached for a washrag. When she saw the reflection of her own expression in the mirror—her smile, her look of contentment, she paused. She was such a fraud, and no doubt Tony would hate her if he ever knew.

She was about to contemplate the possibility of quitting the game before she got in too deep, and then Tony tapped on the door and said, "Come on, honey. Let's get going. If I get to the office soon, I can get my business done and make it an early day. Maybe we can do dinner tonight."

Of course, dinner was not part of the deal, either, but she desperately wanted to give in to him. And she knew by the way her heart jumped at the endearment, she was already in too deep to dig herself out.

She was falling in love with Tony.

7

THE CLICK OF HER HEELS echoed across the faux marble foyer as she headed for the hallway leading to Tony's office. Out of all the Crowns, this was her favorite. Probably because it was in her own hometown; possibly because it was where Tony spent most of his time. This was the office he ran the business from.

She'd been here numerous times, for professional discussions, to meet associates, but never as Tony Austin's lover. Because of that, she'd dressed her best, choosing her most professional outfit. Not by look or by deed did she intend to start the scandalmongers talking. It would be difficult to deal with him in an impassive way, to pretend she hadn't lain naked with him just that morning—that he hadn't done those sinfully wicked, wonderfully arousing things to her.

That she hadn't done some of them back to him.

As she rounded the corner, she met familiar faces and nodded a polite greeting.

"Ms. Anderson," she heard from one woman, and, "How're you doing today, Ms. Anderson?" from a young man.

"Hello, Cathi, George. I'm well, thank you." She kept her responses brief, as was her norm. Tony was

correct when he said she avoided even the simplest relationships. Interacting in a social sphere wasn't easy
for her. She had to work much harder at such relationships than she did when in her business mode. Understanding social etiquette was so much more complicated than working a deal.

She hadn't been here since the night of the party, and
she didn't pay much attention to the remodeling at the
time. But now she did. The carpeting was so soft, the
colors so soothing and gracious, she couldn't help but
admire them. She would have chosen something similar herself. It was just one more way they were alike,
she and Tony.

She opened the glass door and walked to Martha's
desk, then waited while Martha finished up a phone
call.

Be businesslike, Olivia reminded herself, not wanting to take a chance on giving herself away. She was ridiculously nervous, as if she feared Martha would look
at her and notice something different, see some sign of
her new intimacy with Tony. Of course the woman
wouldn't know; it was impossible. But already the situation was far more complicated than she'd ever
thought it could be, and she couldn't help but fidget as
she waited, staring around the office as if she'd never
seen it before.

Finally Martha hung up the phone. "Ms. Anderson.
How nice to see you again."

"Hello, Martha. I need to speak with Mr. Austin. Is
he busy now?"

"He left instructions to notify him right away if you dropped in. Just let me buzz him."

Drat the man, Olivia thought. Couldn't he even remember his own deception? Tony had a long-standing rule: everyone needed an appointment to see him at the office except family and very close friends. Telling Martha such a thing, as if it didn't matter in the least if Olivia interrupted his day, was as good as announcing their sexual relationship.

And then she remembered just how often she'd dropped by to discuss some contract dispute or other, and decided it didn't matter. She had never followed Tony's rules before, not when there was something she wanted.

Of course, usually what she wanted was a better deal, not Tony himself.

The office door opened and Tony stepped out, followed closely by his brother-in-law Brian. She'd almost forgotten that Brian worked in the family business, but seeing him now, dressed in a dark suit and carrying a briefcase, jogged her memory. Two other men exited the office as well, and they all smiled at her. Olivia felt horribly conspicuous. Each of these men managed one of the Crowns; she remembered meeting them at Tony's party the night he'd propositioned her to have his baby.

Trying to work up her best professional expression proved almost impossible, especially given the fact that Tony stood there grinning in an intimate, very telling way. Surely the other men would notice, and then their secret would be revealed.

She was wondering how to react, what exactly to say, when Brian stepped forward and took her hand. "Olivia. It's nice to see you again. I hear you spent the weekend helping Tony baby-sit. Kate was so pleased. She judges everyone's character by how they treat our children, you know, and she claimed right up-front you were a natural."

Olivia drew an appalled blank. Why did everyone keep saying she was a natural? She was hopelessly lost around kids and she knew it. And then it hit her.

Brian had just announced to the entire office that she'd spent the weekend with Tony. She almost groaned and couldn't quite bring herself to look away from Brian and judge the reactions of the other men. Watching Brian, she had the suspicious feeling he'd just done her and Tony in on purpose.

The silence dragged on, and she forced a polite nod. "It was my pleasure," she said, and then flinched at the squeak in her voice.

Brian laughed. "There, you see? Who would consider entertaining three kids overnight a pleasure? Other than Tony, of course. He's a man meant to spawn a dozen, I swear."

Tony laughed. "A dozen? No, thank you. Three was a handful."

Olivia couldn't believe Tony just stood there, joking and laughing and letting the conversation deteriorate in such a way. Did he want everyone to know their business? What had happened to avoiding a scandal?

Brian still held her hand, and with a small tug, he regained her attention. "I keep telling Tony I get a turn now. With our two girls, he'd spend all his time playing house and attending tea parties." Brian cocked an eyebrow. "I don't suppose I can get you and Tony next weekend, can I? The girls would love it, and Kate and I could use the time alone."

Tony shook his head, still grinning, and pretended to stagger with Brian's suggestion. "Give us a month to recuperate, then we'll think about it."

A month? Olivia wouldn't even be seeing him in a month. Two weeks, and that was it. In fact, it was less than two weeks now, since they'd already started on the countdown, as it were.

The thought left her blank-brained for a moment more, and saddened with the reminder that this wouldn't last, that it was so very temporary. When she finally gained enough wit to assess her surroundings, she saw that Tony was dismissing the other two men and saying his goodbyes to Brian. She glanced at Martha, but that busy lady was bent over her computer, typing away. Then she felt Tony's hand on her arm.

In the gentlest tone she'd ever heard from him, he said, "Come on. We'll talk in my office."

Unlike the outer office, this one had solid walls, not glass, and guaranteed privacy, and so she went willingly, needing a moment to gather herself. Tony led her to a padded leather chair and urged her into the seat, then knelt down before her.

"Are you all right?"

She wanted to say that she was fine, but she didn't feel fine. She felt downright wretched. "This is awful."

"What is?"

She gaped at him, refusing to believe he could be so obtuse. "The gossip is probably all over the hotel by now! Everyone will know."

"You're making too much of it, honey. So people will think we're dating? It's not a big deal."

"Not a big deal? You wanted to keep our association private, remember?"

"Our *relationship* is private. No one will know we're trying to conceive a child. And as far as the other, you're attractive, we work together. Why shouldn't people assume we'd share a date or two?"

Olivia bit her lip, his logic irrefutable. "I suppose you could be right."

"I know I am. And as long as my family already knows all about us, you might as well give in and come to Thanksgiving dinner. I'll never hear the end of it if you refuse."

She honestly didn't think she could survive another family get-together. "I really don't..."

Leaning close, Tony framed her face then placed a soft kiss on her lips. "I know it's hard on you, but I'll be there. And after a while, being with a big family won't bother you so much. You might even enjoy yourself.

Besides, the kids are looking forward to seeing you again. And I know you enjoyed them."

"I did." Her answer emerged as a whisper. She was tempted, but also a little afraid. She was losing complete control of the situation, and that hadn't happened to her in years, not since she'd been a child. "I don't want everyone thinking we're seriously involved."

"They'll think whatever they choose whether you're there or not. At least this way, some of their curiosity will die."

"Do you really think so?"

"Sure. Right now they assume I've been trying to keep you a secret. This way, they'll think we're only dating."

Convincing her proved to be much too easy, and Olivia admitted to herself that she actually wanted to go. "I guess you're right. And when the two weeks are over and we stop seeing each other, everyone will just believe we've broken up."

Abruptly Tony came to his feet and stalked toward his desk. He stood there with his face turned away, one hand braced on the edge of the desk and his other hand pressed deep into his pants pocket. He was the perfect study of a man in deep thought, and Olivia wished she could decipher his mood.

Without looking at her, he asked, "How did you come up with this two-week time limit?"

On shaky ground now, she took a second to weigh her answer. "It seemed a reasonable amount of time. If

I was going to conceive, it would probably happen by then."

"So you thought we'd just stop seeing each other, and if and when you turned up pregnant, you'd give me a quick call to break the news to me?"

It sounded very cold, having him spell it out that way. Of course, she knew she wouldn't conceive. "You agreed with that plan, Tony."

"Yeah, well now I don't like it." He glanced over his shoulder at her, then turned away again. "I think I have a better plan."

"And that is?" The mixed feelings of excitement and trepidation settled in her stomach.

"Let's continue to work at conception until we have positive news. If it takes three weeks, or four, what's the big deal? And this way, I'll be able to monitor every second of the pregnancy. You did agree to that, remember."

At that particular moment in time, Olivia wished with all her heart that she wasn't sterile. Spending more time with Tony, allowing him to be such a huge part of her life, would be next to perfection. But since she knew that couldn't happen, she was left floundering for an answer he could accept.

None came to mind, and she stared at his broad back, seeing the rigid set to his shoulders, until finally he asked, "Olivia?"

"There's no guarantee that it'll happen in four weeks, either, Tony. We have to have some time limit. That's only reasonable."

He turned to face her, his expression stern. "Then give me a month."

That was his corporate I'm-the-boss tone, demanding and expecting to be obeyed. She laughed because that tone had never once intimidated her. Teasing him now, she said, "You feel you can come up with sufficient potency in a month, do you?"

He grinned, too, as if her mood had lightened his own. Then his eyes narrowed. "Come here, honey. I have something to show you."

There was a determined set to his jaw, a look of challenge, and Olivia's curiosity carried her quickly to the desk. Spread out over the mahogany surface was a variety of photographs depicting a very posh hotel. "This is a new purchase?"

"Yes." Tony moved the pictures around so she could see them all clearly. "What do you think?"

Olivia studied the photos. There was an immense, elegant banquet room done in burgundy and forest green and gold. One picture showed a pool that seemed to be outdoors, surrounded as it was with foliage and trees and what appeared to be a waterfall, but in fact it was centered within a large glass enclosure. Some of the photos showed ornate chandeliers hanging from many ceilings, and everything seemed to be accented in gold.

"It's beautiful."

"The building itself is actually ancient, and we've kept most of the historic qualities, which will be a draw on their own. But inside, it's been renovated a great deal. It'll be supported by a very upscale clientele, and it's where I thought you might relocate—if you choose—after the baby's born.''

Her eyes widened and she took an automatic step back. Her stomach began to churn with a sick kind of dread. ''I see.''

Tony's jaw tightened and he ran a hand through his hair. ''Actually the shop space is yours whether you conceive or not.''

It took her only a second, and then she shook her head. ''No. Our deal...''

''To hell with the deal!'' He drew a deep breath and shook his head. ''I'm sorry. I feel lousy about this. You see, I'd already considered offering you the space before I talked with you about the baby. But I kept it to myself because I thought it might be an incentive for you to accept my proposition. But now...well, you deserve the space. You're a good choice for the Crown. Our guests always love your shops, so I know you'll do well.''

Olivia felt her head swimming. She tried to think, but it seemed impossible. This had been a horrendous morning all the way around. ''I don't know. It's such a drastic move...''

''It's a move up. A large expansion for your business. The sales potential here will be incredible.'' He waited a heartbeat, then added, ''Of course, the added shop will keep you busy. Having locations so far apart will be time-consuming, leaving little time for anything but work. But that shouldn't be a problem for you.''

She glanced up at the way he said that. His gaze bore into her, hot and intent, waiting. But she didn't know what it was he waited for. Then he insisted, "That's what you want, right?

"I... Yes. I want to grow." Despite everything, she felt a flutter of excitement. The new hotel was exactly the kind of place she eventually wanted to occupy. *Eventually.*

But she knew why Tony was offering it to her. He wanted her to be so busy she wouldn't be able to interfere in his and the baby's life. That hurt. She lifted her chin and gave him a level look. "It's a fantastic opportunity, Tony. But I don't want to get in over my head. The Northwest is so far away…"

"Seattle, to be exact."

He was watching her closely again, his arms crossed over his chest, and she had the feeling he was assessing her in some way. "Seattle." She stepped away, walking around his office to buy herself some time. It was actually an ideal situation, because she'd need to be away from Tony. She had no doubt that once the two weeks was over—and she would somehow have to keep it at two weeks—she would have a terrible time facing him, seeing him and pretending nothing had ever happened between them. The added work would help keep her mind off Tony, off what they had shared. But Seattle!

"I hadn't really considered this in great detail. After all, I've had other things on my mind." She flashed him a quick, nervous smile, which he thankfully returned.

"You can have some time to think about it if you want."

Time. Everything always came down to more time. Or the lack of it. "Yes, thank you." The relief she felt was plainly obvious in her tone.

He put his hand to his jaw, studying her a moment, then went to his office door and turned the lock. It caught with a soft *snick*. When he started toward her again, she could see the intent in his green eyes and she backed up until her bottom hit the desk.

He stopped before her, watching her, waiting. Then, lifting his hands to her shoulders, he gently turned her away from him until she faced the desk. Slipping her purse from her shoulder and setting it on the floor, he said, "Brace your hands flat on my desk."

She obeyed him without thought, her pulse beginning to race. "Tony?"

"I said I wanted to show you two things, honey, remember?"

"I remember." The trembling in her voice should have embarrassed her, but she was too concerned with the way his hands were busy lifting her skirt to pay much attention to anything else. "Tony, I don't think..."

"Shh. There's this quaint custom called a 'nooner.' I think you'll like it."

His fingers slid along the back of her thighs, higher, until they touched the lace edging on her panties. "But, what if Martha knocks?"

"Martha went to lunch," he said, his tone now husky

and deep as he squeezed and petted her bottom. "I don't have any appointments, and at the moment, I'm feeling particularly *potent*." He lightly bit her ear to punctuate that statement.

"Um. I see." His palm slid around to her belly, then dipped into her panties, and she automatically parted her legs. "We can't very well waste your potency, now can we?"

He chuckled, his open mouth pressed to the back of her neck, warm and damp and hungry. And with her heart rapping sharply against her ribs and the sound of his zipper hissing in the quiet of the room, she decided every quaint custom should get its due. And right now, she liked this one very much.

THANKSGIVING DAY rolled around quickly, but Olivia no longer felt any apprehension at joining Tony's family. Over the past two weeks, she'd come to know them all very well. They'd somehow managed to run into her repeatedly, one or the other of them having shown up at her shop whenever she was there ordering, or interviewing new managers for the new location.

It had started with his sister, Kate, who dropped in with the supposed intention of buying lingerie. She did leave with a couple of purchases, but most of her time there was spent chatting with Olivia, getting to know her better and sharing little details of her life.

Kate came again later that week with Lisa, and laughed as she described Brian's reaction to the lingerie Kate had bought.

"I guess I must have let things get a little stale, because when he saw me in that satin teddy with all the cleavage, he nearly fell off the bed."

Lisa joined in the laughter and ordered herself the same teddy in a different color, but Olivia blushed to have such an intimate scene discussed in her presence. In fact, she was blushing most of the time that Lisa and Kate stayed to visit, trying on numerous things and including her in all their "girl talk," as they called it. They didn't pry, didn't ask her anything personal about Tony, but they certainly talked about him.

If there was anything she'd wanted to know, they had the answer, and seemed to relish telling her.

"Tony's played patriarch since our father's death," Kate said, her voice becoming a little more solemn. "He's set himself up in a difficult role, and I for one think he deserves a little fun."

Olivia wondered if she fell under the heading of "fun." Kate and Lisa seemed to think so, given the way they included her.

"It hurt Tony even more than it did the rest of us," Kate continued. "He was the oldest and, even though Dad was always fair, there was a special bond between the two of them. John never had any real interest in the hotels, at least not to the extent Tony did, so it just happened that Tony and Dad spent more time together."

"When he died," Lisa added, "John was so concerned for Tony. But Tony being Tony, he hid whatever grief he felt and dived headfirst into turning the business around. I think he did it as much to keep himself busy as to watch the company grow."

"And he almost cut women out completely. Before that, he'd seemed determined to find a wife. He wanted to be married like the rest of us, and he gave different women a fair chance, though even I'll admit he really hooked up with some impossible choices. Tony is such an idiomatic man, arrogant, but kind. And always in charge. It would take a strong woman to satisfy him."

Lisa laughed, then nudged Kate in the shoulder. "He used to claim he was looking for the perfect woman."

Kate grinned. "And we'd tell him we were already taken."

All three women laughed, and Olivia began to feel some sort of kinship with them. Without thinking, she said, "Well, unfortunately, I'm as far from perfect as he could possibly get."

Kate shook her head. "The idea of perfection exists only in the perspective of the person who's looking— and what that person is looking for. Besides, love has a way of finding perfection in the most unlikely places."

"And anyway," Lisa said, choosing another pair of "barely there" panties, "you and Tony are having fun, he's dating again and the kids all love you. For right now, that's more than enough, don't you think?"

Olivia avoided the context of the question, and said only, "I'm glad the kids approve of me."

"They adore you," Kate insisted. "And the way

those kids worship their uncle Tony, that's a big requirement for any relationship he might have."

Of course, Olivia hadn't told them that her relationship with Tony had a set purpose and a time limit. He'd said to take it one day at a time, and she was doing just that, enjoying herself and storing away the memories so she would never be truly alone again. But her two weeks were rapidly coming to an end, and it wouldn't be fair of her to continue in the deception.

A FEW DAYS LATER, at a different Sugar and Spice location, she was going over some backstock with one of her managers when Brian and John showed up. They looked around the shop with undiluted interest. John appeared to be enthralled, but Brian, unbelievably, had a dark flush to his lean cheeks. Olivia hid her smile.

"So," John called out, striding toward her with his cocky walk and self-assured grin. "There's the lady who's managed to single-handedly put a honeymoon into the daily work week."

Olivia felt her own cheeks heat, and slanted a look at Brian. But he had paused by a rack of a sheer lace camisoles and seemed to be engrossed in examining them.

"Hello, John."

He pulled her close and gave her a big kiss on the cheek. "I do love this place of yours, Livvy, I really do."

He'd affected Maggie's pet name for her, as had all the children. She felt flustered by such an effusive welcome, and tried to gather herself. "I'm glad you approve. Do you have business in the hotel today?"

"Nope. Brian and I are Christmas shopping. Since the ladies have been hanging out here so much, we figured you'd know which things they've shown an interest in."

"Well, yes." There were several items the women had liked, but had hesitated to purchase because they were a bit pricey. She hesitated herself, uncertain of how much they wanted to spend.

Brian took care of that worry for her. "Whatever she wants, I'll buy it."

John laughed at that firm statement. "Poor Brian. Kate has really got you tied up now, doesn't she?"

"You don't see me complaining, do you?"

John gave a mock frown. "I don't know if I like hearing this about my little sister."

"Your sister's not so little anymore, and whatever tendencies ran through the Austin men, she inherited her fair share."

John cast Olivia a look. "Now, Brian, you'll go and spook Livvy if you say things like that."

Olivia had no idea what they were talking about, but she was beginning to get used to the way the men razzed each other. She shrugged and said, "Not at all."

"There, you see? Anyone who knows Tony at all already knows he's a driven man. Just stands to reason that drive would cover every part of his life."

Understanding hit her, and she tightened her lips to hide her smile. Yes, Tony was a "driven" man, always excelling at whatever he did—including lovemaking. She certainly had no complaints there.

Feeling a little risqué herself, she asked, "So it's a family trait, is it?"

John laughed. "Indeed it is. So you see, you with your nifty little shops fit right in. And like all the Austins, Tony goes after what he wants—and doesn't give up until he gets it." She didn't have time to reply to that since he quickly rubbed his hands together and asked, "Now. What does Lisa want? I can hardly wait."

Brian snorted. "Are you sure this shouldn't be *your* Christmas gift?"

Both men paused as if they'd just had the same thought, then reached out to shake hands. "I'll pick what I want, and you pick what you want. At least this year, you won't give me an ugly tie."

"That was a silk tie, you idiot, and very expensive."

"It didn't match anything I own."

The men continued to argue as they each chose what the other would give them for a holiday gift. John picked out a satin Victorian-style corset, then grinned. "I'm going to be a very happy boy on Christmas morning."

Brian held up the gift John would give to him, a snow-white, stretch-lace teddy with attached garters. "Me, too."

The men were so outrageous that Olivia ended up laughing with them and feeling entirely at her ease. Before their shopping spree was over, they'd purchased numerous gifts for their wives, several for themselves, and instructed Olivia to point their wives in the direction of the more risqué items if they mentioned wondering what to get for their husbands. Olivia promised to do just that.

Her manager and the additional clerk had their hands full gift wrapping all the purchases.

They were such an open, loving family, the men so dedicated to their wives, all of them functioning with such unity. And they kept including her. Despite her intentions to stay detached, she found herself feeling a part of things, and actually looking forward to visiting with them again.

This would be the first Thanksgiving she hadn't spent alone since her parents had died, and she was suffering a mix of melancholy and excitement.

TONY ARRIVED RIGHT AT three to collect her. She'd dressed up a little more than usual, wanting to make the most of the day, and when she let him in, he gave a low whistle. "Honey, you'd make the perfect dessert tonight."

With his gaze ranging over her body, she knew the dress had been worth the extra expense. Made of soft black cashmere, it fit her body perfectly, the off-the-shoulder design making it just a bit daring. The hem ended a good two inches above her knees, and she wore heels, which put her on eye level with Tony.

He caught her hand and pulled her close, then bent to press a kiss to her collarbone. "Tony..."

He lifted one hand and palmed her breast, but paused when she sucked in a deep breath. "Did I hurt you?"

She shook her head, unable to catch her breath with him gently kneading her. She felt especially sensitive tonight, her breasts almost painfully tight.

"Your nipples are already hard and I've barely touched you." Tony groaned softly. "What I wouldn't give for an extra hour right now." Reluctantly he released her.

When she turned away to get her coat, he cursed, then mumbled, "If we weren't expected..."

"But we are." She grinned, though she felt every bit as urgent as he did. Even if she had a lifetime, rather than just a few more days, she'd never get enough of having him want her. She shook herself, refusing to think of the self-appointed time limit now. She didn't want anything to spoil this day.

A light snow had started that morning and now, as they stepped outside, Olivia saw that everything was coated in pristine white. The naked tree branches shimmered with it, and it clung to everything, including Tony's dark hair. After he opened the car door for her, she reached up and brushed his cheeks, her fingertips lingering.

"Olivia." Tony leaned down and gave her a melting kiss that should have thawed the snow. He lifted his head, searched her face, then bent to her mouth again. Olivia forgot the weather, forgot that they might be late, and wondered if they could go back inside again.

Then they heard a tapping sound, like knuckles rapping on glass, and they looked up.

At the front door to the apartment building, her neighbors stood watching, huge grins on their faces. When Olivia laughed, they all waved.

"Like Snow White, they're seeing you off with the prince?"

"Hmm. You consider yourself a prince, do you?"

Tony opened her car door and waited for her to get in, then went around to the driver's side. After he'd started the car, he turned to her. "I only meant they're awfully protective of you."

Olivia had to agree on that. "And it's so strange, considering that I've kept to myself. I'm friendly, and I don't go out of my way to avoid them, but neither have I ever sought them out."

"You don't have to. There's just something about you, a genuine feeling, that makes people trust you. And today, with the world what it is, trust is everything."

She looked away. "It's sometimes foolish to trust anyone."

"I trust you."

Oh, why did he have to do this now? "Tony, don't. I don't want to talk about important issues or discuss anything heavy. I just...I want to have fun today."

Glancing at her, he reached for her hand. "And you have fun with my family?"

"I really do. They're all crazy and happy and so accepting, it's impossible not to have fun around them."

She could tell he wanted to say more, but he held his peace. "Okay. But tomorrow we have to talk."

Not really wanting to, but seeing no way around it, she nodded. They would have to talk. Time was running out, and Tony deserved to be set free.

They spent the rest of the drive in silence, holding hands and watching the snow fall.

When they reached his mother's place, Tony walked her to the front door, his arm around her shoulders. The house was decorated with bright Christmas lights, and a hearty wreath hung on the door. Tony tipped up her chin and kissed her. "Smile, sweetheart. Today is just for eating and visiting and, later, making love. Agreed?"

"Of course." She laughed as he pretended to be surprised by her quick agreement.

"Have I spoiled you, Olivia?"

"Shamefully."

"So you'd planned on seducing me later?"

"I had every intention of doing so, yes."

His hand slipped under her coat and lightly caressed her waist. "Does this mean you're wearing something sexy and scandalous and guaranteed to drive me nuts under this dress?"

With wide-eyed innocence, she said, "Of course not."

He frowned, and just as the door started to open, she whispered, "I'm not wearing anything at all."

8

OLIVIA FELT THE FIRST cramps right after dinner, but she ignored them. She was used to such pain, knew it was only her body reminding her that she wasn't what a woman should be. Since she'd had her first period when she was eleven, she'd suffered the cramps. Not normal period cramps, because there was nothing normal about her body's functions.

Sometimes the pains were pretty bad, other times only annoying, but she always managed to function despite their existence, ignoring them until they went away. Except when she'd been a child, and that was when her parents had taken her to the hospital.

She couldn't remember what actual medical term had been given to her condition, but it had to do with her ovaries and the fact they didn't function properly. She'd had surgery to remove a horribly painful mass, and lost one of her ovaries in the process. Since then she was so irregular, she sometimes went several months without menstruating.

Her mother had explained that she likely wouldn't have any children, and Olivia understood why. You couldn't very well conceive with only one ovary, es-

pecially if you didn't ovulate. She wasn't totally igno-
rant about her bodily functions.

There were times when she would have gone to the
doctor, just to make certain her pain was normal, for
her. But being examined by a man when she was still
so innocent and shy had made her dread the thought of
even a routine visit.

Now, as John made a jest and everyone laughed,
Olivia was about to smile when she felt another cramp
and winced instead. Tony leaned toward her. "Are you
all right?"

He'd kept his voice low, thankfully. She didn't want
to disrupt everyone's good time. "I'm fine. I think I just
ate a little too much."

He grinned. "Me, too. I had one too many desserts."
He leaned closer still, his lips touching her ear. "You'll
have to help me work off some calories later. Got any
ideas?"

At the moment, all she wanted was a pain pill. She
patted his arm and got up from the table. "I'll think on
it. Excuse me, please." Picking up her purse, she was
aware of Tony's frowning gaze following her.

When she reached the powder room, she fished out
two over-the-counter pain tablets and swallowed
them, then leaned against the sink. The pain was a little
more acute this time than it normally was. She wondered if the fact that she'd become sexually active had
any bearing on it.

She waited a few minutes more, then left the room,
only to find Tony standing there waiting for her. He

searched her face with his gaze. "What is it, Olivia? What's wrong?"

What was one more lie? She tried surreptitiously to hug her stomach. "I'm feeling a little under the weather, Tony. Maybe I'm catching a cold."

Reaching out, he felt her forehead and then nodded. "You feel a little warm. Why don't we go ahead and leave?"

"No." She didn't want this day to end, not when there were so few days left. "I'm all right."

"You don't look all right, honey. You look like you're in pain."

"It's nothing, I promise."

She sounded a touch too desperate, which made Tony study her a little more thoroughly. "All right. But I want you to sit down and take it easy."

"The women are all helping to clean up the kitchen."

"No, they're not. The men have decided to do it. Now go rest somewhere, okay? And promise me, if you start to feel any worse, you'll let me know."

"I will," she lied, determined to stay for the duration of the family get-together.

But an hour later, the cramps were getting to be too much to ignore, and she couldn't put off leaving any longer. She glanced at Tony and he immediately stood, as if he'd only been waiting for a signal from her. It amazed her that he seemed to read her so easily, that he knew her thoughts and her feelings.

He did a wonderful job of excusing their early departure. Olivia knew, judging by the grin on John's face and the wink Kate sent to her, that everyone thought they were leaving so they could be alone.

When they got into his car, Olivia found that Tony had a similar idea. "I'll take you to my house. I can look after you if you *are* getting sick."

Appalled by such an idea, Olivia shook her head and tried to think of a viable reason to refuse his generous offer. Tending her when she was sick had never been part of the deal. "I'd rather go home, Tony. I'll be more comfortable there."

He glanced at her, then nodded. "All right. I'll grab a few things from my house and stay with you."

Until now she'd managed to avoid having him spend the night or any length of time in her apartment. Generally she met him at the door, and within minutes they would leave. She wanted her home to feel the same once their time together was over, and she knew that would be impossible if he slept in her bed or ate in her kitchen or showered in her bathroom. She would be reminded of him everywhere she looked, and she couldn't let that happen.

She reached over and touched his arm. "Tony, I'm sorry. I really am. But I'd rather be alone. Whenever I've been sick—"

"But you're never sick! You haven't missed a day of work in years."

True. But the cramps had never been this bad before. She bit her lip and looked out her side window. "I'll be more comfortable by myself."

There was an awful silence and she knew she'd hurt

him when that had never been her intent. She felt choked by remorse, but there was no way out, no way to make up for all she'd done, all the lies she'd told.

Finally Tony said very quietly, "I'll take you home. But I want your promise you'll call me if you need anything."

"Of course."

They both knew she was lying.

OLIVIA FINALLY ACCEPTED that something was seriously wrong. The pain had nagged her off and on since she'd come home, and she'd started to bleed. Not heavily, but still, it was an unusual occurrence with her periods so horribly irregular. Then suddenly, at midnight, the pain seemed to explode. She didn't think she could drive herself to the hospital, but as much as she hated to admit it, she needed to go.

This pain no longer seemed familiar; it was nothing like what she was used to dealing with, so sharp she could barely breathe. She had a vague recollection of similar pain when she'd been a child, but it was too hard, feeling as she did, to remember if the two situations were at all the same.

She couldn't disrupt Tony, not after he'd called to check on her and she'd more or less told him not to bother. She'd been curt, as much from the pain as from the struggle to keep from giving in and telling him she needed him. She'd used him enough as it was, and now she didn't know who to turn to.

When she decided she couldn't wait a moment

longer, she pulled a coat on over her pajamas. Bent over, holding her middle, she went into the hallway and knocked on Hilda's door. As usual, one knock had every door on that floor opening, and soon all her neighbors were there, fussing over her, fretting. Very quickly, Hilda reappeared fully clothed, car keys in her hand.

Held between Hilda and kindly old Leroy, Olivia made her way outside. Hilda spoke to those who followed. "I'll call and let everyone know when we've made it to the hospital. If I don't call within a half hour, send a car after us. That snow is really starting to pile up."

Olivia curled into the back seat, and then felt the tears start. It wasn't the pain, but the simple truth that she had good friends and hadn't realized it. Even while avoiding relationships, she'd still managed to form a few. She was only lying to herself when she claimed to be all alone. She was so touched by the sudden revelation, she couldn't halt the tears.

"It's all right, Olivia. Don't worry. I'll have you there in no time." The woman drove like a snail, but Olivia knew Hilda hated the snow. "When we get there, do you want me to call that boyfriend of yours?"

Olivia smiled, hearing Tony referred to as a boyfriend. There was nothing boyish about him, and he was now so much more than a friend. "No. Don't bother him, Hilda. I'll call him myself, later."

"He'd want to be with you, you know."

And then he'd find out what a fraud she was. "No. Please. I don't want to worry him."

Hilda didn't answer.

When they arrived at the hospital, Hilda ran inside, demanding attention, as Olivia struggled to get out of the car. Before she'd even set both feet on the ground, two nurses were there, assisting her into a wheelchair and rushing her in. The questions flew at her, one right after the other, but she was in so much pain she could barely answer. After that, she lost track of events as they ran an endless series of tests.

When a doctor came in and asked her if she might possibly be pregnant, she told him no and briefly explained what she knew of her own medical history. He wrote notes, smiled at her, then went about ordering a pregnancy test. Olivia balked at the idea. She wasn't up to creeping into the bathroom and utilizing their little plastic cups, especially for something that seemed totally unnecessary. But she was too sick to argue. She did as the doctor asked, then crawled back onto the narrow metal bed.

A few minutes later, the doctor leaned against the side rail and gave her a wry look. "Well, Ms. Anderson, it seems you are indeed pregnant."

Olivia stared. "That's impossible."

"I assure you, it isn't." He smiled benignly and went on. "I'd like to do an ultrasound. It will tell us exactly what's going on, why you're having so much pain and bleeding."

Olivia felt numb. Pregnant? She couldn't be pregnant. "But I only have one ovary."

"One is all it takes. Granted, your chances were decreased, but still—it happens."

"But I almost never have periods!"

He patted her hand and stood. "Let's do the ultrasound and then go from there, okay? Try not to worry."

Worry? She was too dumbfounded to worry. And then it hit her and she almost shouted with pleasure. She was pregnant! She would have her own baby, Tony's baby. The pain seemed to lessen with the knowledge, but it was still a reminder that all was not well, and she began praying, wanting this baby so badly she would have promised anything to hold on to it.

It was quite a while before the doctor was standing beside her again. He was a nice enough man, she thought, surprised that she actually felt comfortable with him. In fact, she was anxious to speak with him, to hear how her baby was faring.

He spoke in specific terms for her, making the situation very clear. She wasn't far enough along for the ultrasound to show the baby, but the test confirmed that she had a large cyst on her one remaining ovary—and it had ruptured.

She immediately began to panic, remembering what had happened when she was so young, remembering the surgery, losing an ovary... The doctor pulled up a chair and took her hand.

"Your ovary did rupture, and until your placenta is large enough and produces enough progesterone to maintain the pregnancy, I'll need to give you progesterone and hope it works. Things could still go wrong, and you could lose the baby, but there's no reason to start borrowing trouble yet."

Olivia had never considered herself a weak person. She drew on her strength now, mustering her courage. "I don't need to borrow trouble. It seems I have enough as it is."

"I gather you want to keep the baby."

"Oh, very much! I just never dreamed…"

"When did you lose your other ovary?"

"I was twelve. Not long after I'd started my period. I understood I wouldn't be able to get pregnant. And since my cycle seemed so haywire…"

"It was a common misconception years ago that a woman couldn't conceive with only one ovary, but as you see it is definitely possible." He grinned at her, and she grinned back.

"Yes." Hugging her arms around herself, she asked, "What now?"

"I'd like to keep you here until we can run a few more tests, rule out the possibility of a tubal pregnancy, make certain everything is as it should be. Also, I'd like you to come back a couple of times for blood tests. We'll check the hormone level, which should double in two days if everything is okay. We'll run the test again, just to make sure everything checks out."

He wrote a few notes on her chart, then asked, "Do you have an obstetrician in mind?"

"No." She was in a daze, answering questions she'd never imagined hearing.

"I can recommend someone if you'd like. You should see him right away, then set up frequent appointments until you get past the first three months."

"And after the first three months?"

"Well, then, the risk is greatly reduced."

Olivia hung on to that thought long after the doctor had left. He'd given her codeine for the pain, and it was tolerable now, but she couldn't rest. Her hand remained on her belly, and she couldn't seem to stop crying.

With a little luck and a lot of care, she was going to have a baby.

And there was no way she'd ever give her baby up to anyone—not even Tony.

Olivia worried that thought over and over in her mind, but it always came down to the same thing. She'd have to tell Tony the truth now. She wouldn't keep the baby from him, but neither would she give it up. He had a right to know. She knew he would be a wonderful father, even if he didn't have the situation he wanted, even if he was enraged by her deception.

For one brief, insane moment, she wondered whether Tony would go so far as to offer to marry her, just to get the baby. It was possible, but she wouldn't let that happen. She wasn't the average woman with the average pregnancy. She was more like a miracle.

What would it do to Tony if he married her and she lost the baby? Just the thought had her squeezing her abdomen in a protective embrace; still, it was a very real possibility.

No. Tony needed to find a healthy woman who could give him as many children as he wanted, not just a miracle baby with risks. She'd confess to him, and she would set him free.

It turned out to be the longest night of her life—and the most joyous. A baby, she just couldn't believe she was having a baby.

OLIVIA ARRIVED HOME the next afternoon to a ringing phone. She was feeling much better, more like herself, and she rushed to answer before the caller hung up.

Breathless, weak from her painful ordeal and a sleepless night, she gasped out, "Hello?"

"Where the hell have you been?"

Oh my. She straightened, staring at the receiver in her hand. Tony was in quite a temper. Olivia bit her lip and tried to think of what to say to him.

"Olivia?" There was an edge of near panic to his tone. "Dammit, I'm sorry." He gave a long sigh and she could hear his frustration, could almost see him running his hand through his dark hair. "I was worried, honey. Where were you?"

"I, uh, I had to go out for a little while."

"I've been calling since early this morning. I wanted to make certain you were feeling all right."

That left her blank. She thought they'd agreed he

wouldn't call to check on her. "I'm feeling much better. Tony? Are you busy right now?"

"I'm at the office. Why? Do you need something? You *are* still sick, aren't you?"

He sounded so anxious, she rushed to reassure him. "No, I just..." Her voice dropped as she was overcome with dread, but it was better to get it over with. "We need to talk."

Silence greeted her, and she bit her lip. "Tony?"

"This sounds like a heavy-duty brush-off, Olivia. Is it?"

How could she answer that? How could she possibly explain? She heard him curse, then curse again. "I'll come on over now."

"What?" She didn't want him in her apartment; she wasn't ready to face him. Her night in the hospital had left her looking wan and feeling lifeless. She'd planned to shower and clean up and meet him somewhere. "Why don't we just do lunch?"

"To hell with that. If we need to talk, we'll talk now. Whatever it is you've got planned, I'd rather get it over with. I'll be there in half an hour." He hung up and Olivia sank back onto the couch.

Half an hour to prepare herself. It wasn't much time, but then, from the moment Tony had propositioned her, there hadn't been enough time. She didn't know if a lifetime would be enough.

TONY RAPPED SHARPLY on the door, feeling his frustration ready to explode. The other doors opened, but this time he didn't even look to see who was watching him. He'd almost gotten used to her nosy neighbors who appeared each and every time he came to pick her up. But he was in no mood to be polite right now.

He slammed his fist on the door. "Open up, Olivia."

It didn't matter to him that his behavior was somewhat juvenile. She was dumping him, he was sure of it. *Damn her.* How could she make a decision like this, when he hadn't even made up his own mind about things? He'd thought they were getting closer, thought they might have been able to work through all the difficulties. He'd considered the possibility of offering her a compromise....

But no. She was done giving him time... He raised his hand to bang on the door again, just as it swung in. There stood Olivia.

He opened his mouth, but in the next instant whatever acerbic comment he might have made was forgotten. She looked awful—pale and drawn and tired. Concern immediately replaced all his other emotions. He pushed his way in, forcing her back, closing the door on the curious gazes of her neighbors.

"Olivia?" He caught her shoulders in his hands. "Are you all right, honey?"

"I'm fine." She tried to inch away from him, and he felt his anger renewed. He knew he had to get control of himself. He'd never been concerned with that before. He rarely lost his temper, and never with a woman. He'd never had a relationship with a woman outside the family that had warranted that much emotion. With Olivia, though, he was off balance, bombarded with unique feelings and apprehensions.

He bent to meet her at eye level. "Tell me what's wrong."

She twined her fingers together. "This is very difficult for me. I'm still in shock myself. But... I wanted you to know as soon as possible."

This didn't sound like a rehearsed brush-off. He dropped his hands, but when she staggered slightly, he caught her arm and led her to her couch. "Here, sit down."

She did, and he sat right next to her. "Now just tell me whatever it is. Are you sick?"

"I... I was. Last night." He started to question her, but she said quickly, "And I'm okay now. I promise. It's just that..." Her eyes were huge and dark and filled with uncertainty. Then a small smile flitted over her lips, and she covered her mouth with one trembling hand and whispered, "I'm pregnant."

Tony blinked. Of all the things he'd expected, all the horrible words he imagined... Elation welled, burst. He gave a shout, watching as Olivia blinked back tears, then pulled her close for a hug, rocking her and trying to contain himself. "Don't cry, sweetheart, it'll be all right. I promise."

She was afraid, he understood that now. And he didn't blame her. It was a scary thing to have a baby, but especially so for her, a woman who until recently had never had any dealings with children at all.

Though she was nearly as tall as he, and, as he'd

pointed out to her in one of his less auspicious moments, very sturdy, she felt small and frail. He cradled her close, and then she started to cry in earnest. Could it be she didn't want their time to end? He tipped her chin up and watched as she hiccuped, then wiped her eyes with her fist.

He knew there was a ridiculously tender smile on his face, but he couldn't help himself. She was so sweet, so vulnerable. And then she said in a surprisingly steady tone, "You can't have it."

He tilted his head. "What?"

"You can't have my baby."

He searched her face as realization dawned. She couldn't possibly mean what it had sounded like. "We can discuss—"

"No." She came to her feet, one hand braced on the arm of the couch as if to steady herself. "I have to explain something to you, Tony. When I agreed to your plan, it was because I believed I couldn't have children. When I was very young, I lost an ovary due to a condition called PCO, polycystic ovaries. My periods have never been normal, or even close to regular, and so I didn't think I could conceive. I believed I could make love with you without any risk of pregnancy, otherwise I never would have agreed to give you the baby."

He was frozen with shock, what she was saying too unbelievable to accept. "Then why...?"

She laughed harshly, and again covered her mouth. "Look at yourself. You're a very desirable man. You'd never shown any interest in me before, and most of my reasoning was true. I wanted to know what lovemaking was all about, with a man I admired and could trust."

"You lied to me?"

She choked on a sob. "Yes."

Slowly, feeling as if his body wouldn't function properly, Tony came to his feet. She hadn't dressed today as she normally did. Today she was wearing a long casual caftan, and her feet were bare; her hair was brushed but unstyled. Every time he thought he'd figured her out, she changed.

And this change was killing him.

"You used me for sex."

Wrapping her arms around her middle, she nodded. "I'm so sorry."

"Sorry?" His voice had risen to a shout, and she flinched. It hit him then: she was pregnant. With his baby. He didn't want to upset her, not knowing what it might do to the baby, and he fought hard to regain some calm. "This is why you kept telling me you might not conceive."

"Yes."

"And why you insisted on the two-week time period."

Again, she said only, "Yes."

"But everything backfired on you. Because you are pregnant?"

"I am. It's definite." Her lips trembled when she drew in a deep breath. "I wouldn't have realized it on my own for some time yet, but then I got...sick, and the doctor did a test, an accurate test, and now I know I'm going to have a baby."

His jaw tightened. "Must have been one hell of a shock for you."

Instinctively she placed her hand on her belly. "It was." And there was that small smile again, as if she was glad, but trying desperately to keep her happiness to herself.

"So," he asked, not really wanting to, but having to know, "how do I fit into all this? It is my baby, too."

She turned away and walked to an end table, straightening a lamp shade, flicking at a speck of dust. He looked around and realized he hated her apartment. It was so like the business persona she presented to the world—detached, immaculate, no softness or giving anywhere. The place could have been empty and not seemed any less cold.

"I want you to take part in everything, if you want to."

Barking a rough laugh, he caught her shoulder and turned her back to face him. "If I *want* to?" Her eyes opened wide and he almost shook her. "I was the one who *wanted* the baby, not you! You had the grand five-year-plan, remember?"

Hands curled into fists, she jerked away. "Only because I didn't think I could have a baby! But I can, and I want this one."

"What about work? How are you going to raise a baby by yourself?" He knew he was being unfair, asking her questions she couldn't possibly have found the answers to yet, but at the moment, it didn't matter. He wanted to hurt her just as she'd hurt him.

And judging by the stricken look on her face, he had.

He tilted his head back and closed his eyes, silently counting to ten. Then he faced her. "Olivia, be reasonable. Do you have any idea how difficult it is to be a single parent?"

"I suppose I'll find out, won't I?"

He almost laughed, she looked so much like herself, digging in, ready to do battle. He rubbed his chin and studied her. "I could take you to court, you know? I can provide for the baby in a way you never could. I can give him things, my time and attention..."

"What if it's a girl?"

"You don't remember me telling you it wouldn't matter? I thought I was clear on that."

Abruptly she dropped back onto the couch, her face in her hands. "Don't do this, Tony. Don't make things more difficult for me. Please!"

His chest hurt, seeing her look so defeated. All her bravado had just vanished in a heartbeat. He sat beside her and awkwardly tried to find the right words. "I *will* be a part of the baby's life, Olivia."

She jerked around to face him, her expression anxious and fierce. "Of course you will be! I wouldn't keep you from him. Or her, or..." She paused, and then grinned past her tears. "Oh, Tony, I'm having a baby!"

She was crying and laughing, and he couldn't help but hug her to him. She started babbling, her words almost indistinguishable mingled as they were with her sobs.

Keeping her face close to his chest, she said, "I never, ever thought this was possible. And I swear, I'll be a good mother. I didn't mean for this to happen, and I know it wasn't what you wanted. It wasn't even what I wanted. But I won't tie you down. I promise. You can see the baby whenever you want, be as close to it as you want. Your life doesn't have to change, just because I want to remain the baby's mother. I'll figure out some way to keep my business going and take care of the baby, too. And you'll be the father, so you can—"

"Watch the baby for you while you go on about your business?" They had agreed the baby would be his, but now she planned to keep the baby, and use him again to make it easier on herself? He leaned back, holding her away from him.

She swallowed in the face of his renewed anger. "That wasn't what I was going to say."

"No? But you're seeing yourself with only half a problem, right? After all, I can support you both while you go about your plans to expand the business. And whenever the baby is inconvenient, I'll be a built-in baby-sitter. How could I ever refuse, when I'd wanted this child so much?"

She seemed to go perfectly still, not breathing, not moving so much as an eyelash. Then a placid, business smile came to her mouth, and he didn't like it, didn't like the way she'd pulled herself together and back into that protective shell of hers. It was the way she always looked during a business meeting, the look that had led him to believe she had no sensitivities, no vulnerabilities. He knew now that it was a sham.

Her back was very straight, her chin lifted when she said, "You thought I'd start using you that way? Not at all. I need nothing from you. I've never needed anything from anyone. The baby and I will be just fine."

"Olivia..."

"I think you should go now."

"We're not through talking."

"Yes, we are. I've told you all I have to tell you. Whether or not you choose to take part in the baby's life is up to you now."

He glared at her, his jaw so tight it ached. "You know damn good and well I want this baby."

"Fine." She stood, managing to look somehow regal and serene despite her obvious fatigue and whatever illness had plagued her. "When he or she is born, I'll let you know."

Then she went to the door and opened it, waiting for him to leave.

And he did, only because he was so angry, he was afraid he'd upset her again if he stayed, and he couldn't believe that would be good for the baby. Feeling numb and sick to his stomach, he stomped out to his car and then sat there. Damn her, she'd thrown him for a loop this time.

He realized there was still so much he didn't know about her—and despite everything, he wanted to know. She'd actually had some sort of surgery when she was young that made her believe she couldn't get pregnant.

And she'd pretended otherwise just so she could make love with him.

It seemed absurd, especially now that she'd been trapped by her own ridiculous plan. But he wasn't giving up yet. Olivia always wanted to run things, in business and in private. It was part of her nature to take charge and make all the decisions. She was pushy and arrogant and in the general course of things, very fairminded.

But not this time.

Damn, he knew he should have stuck to his original plan. He should never have gotten involved on a personal level with Olivia Anderson. He hadn't gotten the baby he wanted so badly; he hadn't gotten anything at all.

Nothing except a broken heart.

9

"SO WHEN ARE YOU going to marry her?"

Slowly, wishing he didn't have to deal with this right now, Tony laid his papers aside. "I'm not."

John placed both palms on his desk and leaned forward to glare at him. "And why the hell not? She's perfect for you."

Perfect? Nothing felt perfect. It had been two weeks since he'd seen Olivia. He'd tried dropping in on her shops a couple of times, hoping to appear casual about seeing her since his pride was still bruised. He would have conjured up a business excuse, but in truth, he'd half hoped that seeing him again would give her a change of heart, that she would want him again, even though she was pregnant. But she hadn't been there.

He'd called her apartment once or twice, but each time he'd gotten her answering machine. No doubt she was busy organizing things for the new shop she would open.

And that thought made him angry all over again.

He glanced up at John, then back to his desk full of files, trying subtly to give the hint that he was busy. "It's none of your business, John."

"You've been moping around long enough. Hell,

Mom's worried about you, Kate's worried about you. Why don't you just accept the inevitable and admit you love her?"

"Because she lied to me, that's why!" He hadn't meant to shout, but he'd had no one to talk to, and he was ready to explode with the effort of trying to understand Olivia and his own feelings.

John straightened, looking startled by Tony's display of temper. "Lied to you about what?"

Wishing he'd kept his mouth shut now, Tony shook his head. "Why don't you mind your own business?"

Instead John propped a hip against the desk. "Was it a big lie, or just a little lie? Now don't glare at me. I'm trying to help."

"If you want to help, find me a woman as perfect as Lisa."

A look of stunned disbelief crossed John's face, then he burst into hysterical laughter. "Lisa? Perfect? You've got to be kidding."

"She's perfect for you. The two of you never fight. And I know damn well she'd never lie to you."

"We fight all the time, actually. I enjoy it. And it gives me a good excuse to make up to her." He winked, which confounded Tony. "As far as lying...Lisa would never lie to me. But I lied to her once, and it was a doozy."

Tony laid aside the file he'd just picked up and stared. "When was this?"

"Before we were married. Almost ruined things, and that's a fact. But Lisa, bless her heart, didn't give up on me. She got madder than hell, then she schemed, and before I knew it, I was apologizing and begging her to marry me. As it turned out, she wasn't so upset over what I'd lied about, as she was that I'd lied at all. Is that true with you and Livvy?"

Tony considered the question a moment. Was he mad that Olivia had used him for sex, or that she didn't appear to want him now? He figured he could forgive her anything if she loved him, but... He shook his head, not really coming up with an answer. "I don't suppose you'd care to tell me what you lied to Lisa about?"

"Actually...no." He grinned. "It's history, and now I'd never lie to her about anything any more than I'd ever hurt her."

"But you two fight?" Tony was intrigued by the idea; he'd always thought his brother had the perfect marriage.

"All the time. Hell, you know me, Tony. Did you really think anyone could live with me without losing their temper on occasion?"

"And Kate and Brian?"

"They've had their share of whoppers. Kate can be a real pain, you know that. And she claims Brian is far from perfect. If you love Olivia, it won't matter."

Tony narrowed his eyes, considering what John said, but the big difference was that Olivia didn't appear to love him. "I don't know."

John slammed a palm on the desk. "I don't get it! She's a sexy lady. Smart. Sweet. The kids love her. The women love her."

Tony ignored him, going back to his papers and pretending a great interest in them, even though his eyes wouldn't seem to focus on a single line.

John crossed his arms over his chest and glared. "She is sexy, you know. Very sexy."

The paper crumpled in Tony's fist. He slanted his gaze up at his younger brother and asked in a growl, "Just what do you think you're doing, noticing if she's sexy or not?"

"Do I look blind? Olivia is one of those intriguing cool-on-the-outside, burning-up-on-the-inside kind of ladies. Every guy who looks at her knows it. It's just that usually a guy's too afraid to get close enough to her to see just how sexy she is. She can be damn formidable as I remember it. Of course, after you got her to soften up a bit, it's more noticeable."

"Oh, that's just dandy." She no longer wanted him, but he'd managed to show the world how appealing she was? He didn't need to hear that.

"You don't have to worry about me or Brian. You know we're both well satisfied in our own marital bargains, but..."

"Brian, too?"

"He's not blind, either, big brother."

Tony threw the papers aside and shoved his chair back, then took an aggressive step toward John. He felt ready to chew nails, but John only shook his head.

"Look at you. This is pathetic. Give up and tell her you love her and you want her back."

Tony narrowed his eyes and against his best intentions, blurted, "She dumped me, you ass. Not the other way around."

It was almost funny the look that flashed over John's face. Obviously this possibility hadn't occurred to him. He asked simply, "Why?"

Shaking his head and stalking around the office, Tony knew he'd already said too much. No way would he ever confide in anyone—even his brother—the extent of Olivia's perfidy. "Go away and leave me alone, John."

John didn't budge an inch. "I don't get it. She seemed crazy about you. I was sure of it."

Crazy about him? Tony stared, wondering if it could have been possible.

Then John demanded, "What did you do to her to make her dump you? Did you yell at her over this lying business?"

This time he did laugh, but there was nothing humorous in the sound. What had he done? Made love to her, as per her request, giving her pleasure, giving her his baby.

Then he'd accused her of using him for money. It had been his anger talking, but still, he shouldn't have made such a ridiculous claim. Sex, yes, but Olivia would never use anyone for money. God, she'd spent her life proving her independence, isolating herself, facing each day alone.

But now she'd have the baby. His baby.

He cursed again, aiming his disgust at John. But it was a wasted effort. John only dropped into a chair and looked thoughtful. "I think we need to figure this one out."

"I need to get back to my work." He said it through gritted teeth, wanting privacy to wallow in his misery, but John shook his head.

"I don't understand why, if you want her, you don't just woo her."

"Woo her? *Woo* her? What kind of word is that?"

"An appropriate kind. Olivia must need something you haven't given her yet. When I was dating Lisa, I always thought I was saying the right thing, and it always turned out to be the wrong thing."

Brian opened the door just then and walked in to hear John's statement. He grinned. "You have a knack for saying the wrong thing. So what else is new?"

John turned and without a single hesitation, explained the situation to Brian. Tony threw up his hands and dropped back into the chair behind his desk. He listened as the two men discussed his life as if he weren't even in the room. Damn interfering...at least his mother and sister didn't know.

No sooner did he have the thought, than Kate came storming in.

"What did you do to Olivia?"

Tony leaned back in his chair and closed his eyes.

Again, John began to explain. Tony tried to tune them out, but then Kate said, "Oh. When I talked to her, she only said that they weren't seeing each other anymore."

"You talked to her?" Tony asked, sounding anxious in spite of himself. "When?"

"Just this morning. She sounds awful. Not at all like herself."

"What do you mean? Is she still sick?" He was aware of their looks, how they all exchanged glances, but at the moment, he didn't care.

"I don't know anything about her being sick, Tony. I assumed she was heartbroken. But then, I thought you had broken things off. I mean, it was obvious she was crazy about you."

There it was again. Tony leaned forward and said, "Why does everyone keep saying that! The woman dumped me."

"What did you do to her?" asked Kate and Brian together.

Tony had had enough. He came to his feet in a rush and said to the room at large, "I'm going out for lunch."

John grabbed his arm before he could leave the room. "I've always thought you were an intelligent man, Tony. But right now, you're acting pretty dumb. Don't sit around here sulking. Go fix things with her."

"And how am I supposed to do that?"

John slapped his shoulder and grinned. "As I said, you're smart. You'll think of something."

IT TOOK TONY a few more days to come up with a solid plan. But once he did, he couldn't believe he hadn't thought of it sooner. It was perfect, probably the only ploy that would work with Olivia.

He would appeal to her business ethics.

He tracked her down at the downtown shop where she was busy stringing white twinkle lights in the front store window that faced the lobby. She stood on a small stool, a smile on her face, looking beautiful and healthy and not at all like a woman pining away for a man. He almost balked, but then she looked up and met his gaze and her smile vanished. Her dark eyes took on a wary look.

He approached her and took her hand, helping her to step down from the stool. "Hello, Olivia."

"Tony. What brings you downtown?"

"I was looking for you, actually."

That wary look intensified and she nervously brushed her hands together. "Oh?"

"We have some things to discuss, I think. Don't you?" He kept his tone gentle, not wanting to upset her before it was absolutely necessary.

"I...I suppose we do." She turned and called to her assistant. "Finish hanging these lights, will you, Alicia? I'll be in my office."

Without a word to him, she started toward the back of the shop. This location was smaller than the one they'd met in before, but he liked it. There were the red bows and garlands strung around the shop and Tony wondered if she decorated her own home at all. Doubtful. Her apartment was utilitarian to the point of being depressing.

This year, he hadn't decorated, either. It just hadn't seemed important.

She closed her office door after he'd stepped inside, then went to sit behind her desk. There was only one other chair in the room, a plain wooden chair, and Tony pulled it forward. "How have you been, Olivia? Kate mentioned that you seemed ill."

She looked frightened for a second, then she visibly relaxed. "Morning sickness, I'm afraid. Although it hits me at the oddest times, not just in the morning."

Perfect, Tony thought, knowing he couldn't have asked for a better opening. "Any other changes you're noticing?"

Looking anxious, she smiled and said, "You know, there are. Small things, but it's amazing how the baby is making itself known. Even though I'm not very far along yet."

"What kind of things?" He held her gaze, refusing to let her look away.

She flushed, then shook her head. "Nothing big. Just...little things."

"But I want to know." He added gently, "That was part of our deal, remember?"

Olivia stiffened at the reminder of their original bargain. "What are you talking about?"

It took all his control to look negligent, to hide his growing anticipation. If she guessed at his ulterior motives, she'd throw him out on his ear. He picked up a lacy slip lying on the desk and pretended to examine it. "You agreed to allow me to view all the changes—if you got pregnant. I realize now of course that you only made the deal because you thought it would never come to this. But I've given it a lot of thought. And I've decided you should be fair-minded about the whole thing."

Her face was pale now and her hands were clenched together. "I already told you how sorry I am about all that, Tony. But I'm keeping my baby."

"I'll want visitation."

"I offered it to you."

"And," he went on, as if she hadn't spoken, "I'll want to pay for half the baby's bills. As to that, I should pay for half your medical bills as well."

"No!" She was out of her seat in as instant and leaning over the desk to glare at him. "I told you, I want nothing from you."

"And I believe you. But it's my right to pay half."

"But it's my body, my baby!" Then she stumbled back, realizing what she'd said. Tony merely waited, and she drew several deep breaths. "Okay. It's your baby, too. And when it's born, if you want to take part of the pediatrician's expenses on yourself, that's fine. Why should we argue? But my bills are my own."

"I could take you to court, you know."

She gaped at him. "You'd sue me to get half my bills?"

He shrugged. "That, and to get you to honor the bargain we made."

Feeling behind herself for her chair, she dropped down and concentrated on taking several deep breaths. Her face was pale, her eyes huge. "You're go-ing to take the baby from me?"

Tony felt like a monster. He stood up and went around the desk, then turned her chair toward him. Kneeling, he took her hands in his and held them tightly. "Do you honestly think I'd do that to you, Olivia?"

She shook her head and her hair tumbled over her shoulders. "No. But you said..."

"We made other deals, sweetheart." He kept his tone low and soothing. "Don't you remember?"

Her gaze became wary.

"I want to be a part of the pregnancy as well as the birth. You promised me I could observe all the little changes, watch you as the baby caused changes in your body. I want to do that, Olivia. I want to know every little thing that occurs."

"But...everything is different now."

"No. The only thing that's different is that you've admitted you lied to me, and you want to keep the baby. The rest of our agreement should stand." He squeezed her fingers again and stared into her stunned gaze. "It's the least you could do."

He could tell she was considering it, thinking about it. His gaze dropped to her breasts and he whispered, "I bought a book that detailed all the changes. One of the first things to happen is your breasts should get tender and swollen." He glanced up and was caught by her wide dark eyes. "I remember now, the last time we made love, you seemed especially sensitive."

Her chest heaved as she watched him, and then she nodded.

"Ah. So they are swollen?"

Licking her lips, she nodded again. "A little."

"And they're tender?"

"Yes." Her voice was a barely discernible whisper, husky and deep and shaky.

"I want to see."

"Tony..."

The way she groaned his name did things to him, things that shouldn't be happening right now, not while he was trying so hard to get the upper hand. He rubbed his thumb over her knuckles and whispered to her. "Shh. It'll be all right. I'm just curious. You know how much this has meant to me. Can't you give me at least this much?"

"But I thought you'd find another woman."

The thought of touching anyone other than Olivia was somehow repugnant. He didn't want another woman. Even if he went the rest of his life without a child that would be solely his, he wouldn't want anyone but her. The idea was staggering, but true.

"No. I don't think that's necessary." He released her hands and stood, needing to put some space between them before he embarrassed himself by making declarations that would be better left unsaid. At least for now. "We'll have this baby, and that's enough to deal with. Hell, this is far more complicated than I'd ever intended."

He had his back to her and didn't hear her rise, but

then she was touching him, and he turned. She stood looking up at him, her expression earnest. "I'm so sorry, Tony. Honestly. I never meant for any of this to happen. It seemed like such a simple plan to me."

Touching her cheek, he smiled. "Nothing about you is simple, honey. You're the most complex woman I know."

She looked crushed. "I've really messed things up for you, haven't I?"

She'd made him happier than he'd ever imagined being, but he didn't tell her that. "Things aren't just as I'd planned them, but I *will* get my child. I'll just be sharing it with you." He shoved his hands into his pockets to keep from touching her again. "But it would help if you'd abide by the agreement as much as possible. You knew from the start how I felt about things."

She nodded miserably, and he almost apologized for heaping on the guilt, but she deserved it for her deception. And it was the only way he could think of to reach his goal.

"Then you'll agree? You'll let me observe the changes and take part in everything?"

She turned away and wrapped her arms around herself. "What exactly do you mean by 'taking part'?"

"I want to attend your doctor appointments. If there are any sonograms taken, I want to be there so I can see whatever you see. When the doctor listens for a heartbeat, I want to hear it, too."

Her shoulders slumped in relief. "That's no problem."

"I also want to know about every spell of morning sickness. I want to see your ankles if they swell." Without his intention, his voice went husky. "And feel if your breasts are tender."

She shuddered, and he wanted her right then, so badly he could hardly breathe. "I've seen you before, Olivia, so it won't be a breach of your privacy. I've touched you..." He had to stop to draw his own breath, his lungs feeling constricted, his stomach tight with need. "I know your body, how it looks and how it feels. It'll be easy for me to see every tiny change. Will you let me?"

She nodded very slowly, and his pulse quickened. But he wanted to be sure. "Olivia?"

"Yes." She faced him, her cheeks flushed, her eyes bright. "Yes. That's the least I can do."

He recognized the signs of arousal in her expression and it took a moment before he was able to speak. "I can come over tonight."

"I'd rather..."

"I know. You don't want me in your apartment." She looked surprised, and he gave her a wry smile. "I realized after I left there the last time, you've always avoided having me in your home. That was because you had no intention of having my baby, of course, and you wanted to keep your life separate from mine. You didn't want me invading your inner sanctum."

With a guilty flush, she nodded.

"But now you are having my baby, and I will be visiting there, if for nothing else than to pick up the child. So it doesn't really matter anymore, does it?"

"I suppose not."

She looked reluctant as hell, and he almost grinned. *I've got you now*, he thought, knowing he was moving in on her, and knowing she didn't like it. He said, "How about six o'clock?"

"I suppose I should be finished by then."

"Good." He didn't want to go, but he decided to leave before she changed her mind. "I'll see you then."

OLIVIA STRAIGHTENED her hair again, then stepped away from the mirror. Tony was five minutes late, and she was a nervous wreck. She couldn't believe he was doing this, but she was so glad. She'd missed Tony horribly, the days stretching on endlessly. She'd wanted so many times to tell Tony of all the little changes she'd noticed. Not even work had filled the void—a situation she had never encountered before.

Until now.

When the knock sounded on the door, she jumped, then raced to answer it. She didn't want to have to deal with her neighbors today; they'd been hovering over her ever since that night at the hospital. While she appreciated their concern, she didn't want Tony to know about the risks involved with the pregnancy.

But when she opened the door, Tony stood there surrounded by familiar faces. He gave her an ironic grin, said goodbye to all her neighbors and stepped inside. As she was closing the door again, Hilda called out, "You take good care of her now, you hear? I don't want to be making any more trips to the hospital."

Though she could have wished it otherwise, Olivia knew Tony had heard every word. He stared at her, then started to open the door again—to question Hilda she was certain.

"Don't, Tony."

"What the hell was that about the hospital?"

She tried to think of some excuse to give him, but he grabbed her shoulders and gave her a slight shake. "No more lies, Olivia. Dammit, just once give me the truth."

She flinched at his tone, and at his right to doubt her. "I'm sorry. I just didn't want to worry you."

"Worry me about what? Is the baby okay?"

"The baby is fine." She rushed past him to the end table to pick up a recent sonogram picture. "This is the baby."

Tony looked at the odd black and white picture, frowned, then asked, "Where?"

Olivia laughed in delight because his reaction was so much like her own had been. "You can't really see the baby, it's so tiny. In fact, right now, it's only about half an inch long. But did you know, by about eight weeks, it will already be getting fingers and toes?"

Tony stared, then a huge smile broke out over his features. "Fingers and toes, huh?"

Olivia held up the picture and pointed out what she did know, showing Tony her womb and explaining the dark shadows as they'd been explained to her. "My doctor is very big on ultrasound, especially since I didn't believe I could conceive."

"Okay, start with that. What exactly happened to you? And how is it you got pregnant when you thought you couldn't?"

She was so thrilled to have someone to talk all this out with, she took Tony's hand to lead him to the couch before she could think better of it. She explained her specialized problem at length, and Tony asked a million questions.

"But what happened the other night? Why did you go to the hospital?"

Feeling her way carefully now, not wanting him to know of the risks involved, she said simply, "I had another cyst on my ovary. It was causing me some pain." And before he could question that, she added, "But that's a good thing, because otherwise I wouldn't have gone to the hospital, and I wouldn't have known I was pregnant. Heaven only knows how far along I would have gotten before I realized what was happening."

He searched her face, his concern obvious. "You're sure you're okay now?"

"I'm positive. They took very good care of me. I felt wretched for a few days, and if you check, you'll find I missed a few days of work. But now, other than the morning sickness, I feel great."

"You don't look pregnant."

He was staring down at her body, and she felt a flash of heat. Clearing her throat, she tried to distract herself from thinking things she had no business thinking.

"According to the book I bought, I won't start picking up any real weight until after the first three months."

"But you said you've noticed signs?"

This was the tricky part. "My skin is different. I don't need to use as much moisturizer. My hair is different, too. I've had to switch shampoos to get it to lay right." She laughed. "I have unbelievable cravings, and I have to go to the bathroom more."

"And your breasts are swollen and tender."

"Well...yes." She had hoped to slip that in with all the rest, but he hadn't given her a chance.

He took her hand and pulled her to her feet. She stared up at him, feeling her heart pound, her temperature rise. In a low, tender voice he said, "I want to see, Olivia. Take your shirt off for me."

10

OLIVIA SWALLOWED HARD and closed her eyes. Not for the life of her could she unbutton the pale flannel blouse she wore. Then she felt Tony take her hand and her eyes flew open again.

"Let's go in the bedroom so you can lie down. It'll be easier for me to...examine you that way."

Examine her. Her heart was tripping, her stomach pulling tight, and yet she let him lead her to her bedroom—a place he'd never been before—without a single complaint. She knew, in her own heart, she wanted him to touch her, to look at her. But she didn't think she could admit such a thing. Not after how badly she'd blundered so far. It was a wonder Tony would even talk to her, much less want to touch her.

She sat on the edge of the bed when he gently pressed her down, and then his hands were on her shoulders, urging her back. She squeezed her eyes shut and she could hear her own breath.

His knuckles brushed against her as he slowly unbuttoned her top and parted the material. Her bra was new, sturdier than those she usually wore, and it had a front closure that Tony deftly flicked open. He brushed the cups aside and then she felt nothing but the cool air on her breasts.

"Olivia. Open your eyes."

She did, feeling foolish, and saw that he was just standing there, looking down at her, his gaze intent. She started to cover herself, but he caught her hands then sat beside her on the bed. "You are much fuller."

She could hear the amazement in his gravelly tone, and she said, "I'm going to breast-feed when the baby is born."

His gaze shot to her face. "Are you?"

"Yes. I've been reading a lot of books about it." Her own voice crackled and shook in nervousness and arousal, but she ignored it. Tony was interested in all this, and she did owe it to him to keep him apprised of everything.

He lifted a hand and with one finger followed the tracing of a light blue vein to the edge of her nipple. She sucked in a deep breath, but he seemed unaware of her predicament as he cupped her fully in his palm, weighing her. When his thumb touched her nipple she shuddered.

"You're a lot more sensitive, aren't you?" There was awe in his whispered question, and she could only nod her head.

"Olivia?" His hand rested low on her midriff now, and she watched as he unbuttoned her tan wool slacks and slid the zipper down. "I want to see all of you." He tugged her pants off, and when she saw how his hands shook she had to bite back a groan.

She lay there, legs slightly parted, her upper body framed by the shirt that still hung from her arms, while Tony's gaze, so hot and fierce, roamed all over her. When he bent to press his cheek to her belly, she couldn't stand it a second more. She curled up to wrap her arms around him, and the tears started.

"Shh. Sweetheart, don't cry."

He held her close, gently rocking, but the tears wouldn't stop. "What is it, Olivia? Did I hurt you?"

As if he ever would. She shook her head and squeezed him tighter.

"I need you, Livvy. I want to make love to you."

She didn't need any encouragement beyond that. She shifted so she could find his mouth, then kissed him hard, clasping his face between her hands and biting his lips.

He laughed, then groaned and in a heartbeat he was over her, kissing her everywhere, kicking off his shoes.... Olivia struggled with his shirt until finally he sat up and stripped off his own clothes. As he lowered himself on top of her again, he said, "Tell me if I hurt you."

"You won't. You couldn't. Please, Tony, I missed you so much."

His hand slid down her belly and started to stroke her, but she curled her fingers around his erection and he froze. "Damn, sweetheart, don't do that. I won't be able to..."

"I don't want you to. Just make love to me, Tony. Now."

His gaze locked on hers for a long moment, and then his fingers were parting her, preparing her. She was already wet and ready for him, and when he lifted his damp fingers to his mouth, she groaned, watching him lick the taste of her from his hand, seeing the heat in his eyes. She pulled him over her, kissing him wildly, opening her legs wide and he gently pushed inside her until she groaned and wrapped herself around him. It was excruciatingly sweet and slow and hot, and it was all she could do not to tell him she loved him. He held her face still and kissed her as she climaxed, letting her suck his tongue, then whispering to her in a voice so low she couldn't hear what he was saying. He pressed his face into her throat and gave a deep, hoarse groan, and she held him, stroking his back until his breathing had calmed.

TONY PUSHED HER DAMP HAIR away from her face, smoothed her eyebrows, and all the while, she could see him thinking. It was the awkward moment after, and she wanted to put it off, but there was no place to hide. Before he said it, she knew what was coming.

"Marry me."

Oh God, it hurt. She shook her head as fresh tears rolled down her cheeks, as much denying the words as denying him. "I can't."

"Why?"

She'd known he would ask. Tony didn't like being refused—for any reason. She looked at him squarely and went on the defensive. "Why do you want to marry me?"

He gave her a disgruntled frown and shoved himself away from her, sitting on the edge of the bed with his naked back to her. "We're having a baby, and I can't keep my hands off you. Don't you think marriage would be a good idea?"

The disappointment was crushing, but she kept her tone level, not letting him see how much his reply had hurt. "You planned all along for us to have a baby, but you didn't want to marry me. As I recall, you were appalled when I first misunderstood that to be your intention."

"That was when I thought the baby would be mine alone."

"I see." She scooted up in the bed and began refastening her clothing. Her bra left her stymied for a moment and required all her attention. As she buttoned her shirt, she watched him. "I've told you I'll share the baby with you. I would never deny you your child, or deny the child a father. And you'll make an excellent one. You can take on as big a role as you wish."

He started to say something fierce—she could tell by the frown on his face—but the knocking at her front door stopped him. His expression turned comical for a moment and then he cursed. "I don't believe this, I really don't. I'd have thought we'd be safe here, at your place."

He moved over on the bed as she jumped up and

started pulling on her slacks. "At least we know it can't be my family this time."

Olivia shook her head, glad of the reprieve, regardless of who it was. "I can't imagine who would call on me."

Tony lounged back, gloriously naked and unconcerned by that fact. "That's right. You avoid all relationships, don't you?"

His sarcasm was especially sharp after the tender way he'd made love to her. She slanted him a look as she headed out of the room, then had to force herself to look away from the sight of his blatant masculinity.

"Do me a favor and stay put, okay?" She didn't wait for an answer, but pulled the bedroom door shut and went to see who was knocking. It had to be one of her neighbors, she thought, trying to smooth her hair and wipe her eyes dry at the same time. She was wrong. She opened the door to find a good portion of Tony's family standing in the hallway, exchanging pleasantries with her neighbors, who of course had opened their own doors to see who was visiting the building.

Kate was the first one to notice Olivia. Grabbing her and giving her a big hug, Kate explained, "We were out shopping and realized we hadn't invited you to Christmas dinner yet."

Lisa stepped forward with John and Brian in tow, and Olivia had no choice but to move out of the way so they could enter. "The kids would love to see you again. They've been asking after you."

John grinned. "And Tony would love to see you, too, I'm sure."

Lisa poked her husband in the ribs. "John. You promised you'd behave yourself."

"I am behaving. I'm not telling her what a sullen ass Tony's been lately, am I?"

Olivia felt her stomach start to churn. It was always this way. The nausea would hit her at the most inopportune moments, usually when she was on her way to work or while she was at one of the shops, with customers all around.

Now, with Tony's family surrounding her, had to be the worst timing of all. She cringed, then laid a hand to her stomach, praying her belly would settle itself.

Kate stepped forward and put her arm around Olivia, misunderstanding her distress. "We don't mean to upset you, Olivia. But we really would love to have you. And in all honesty, the kids do ask after you. I think they miss you."

Olivia was thinking it couldn't get any worse when Tony came on the scene. "No fair, sis," he said, "using the kids as bait."

Everyone turned to stare at her bedroom doorway, where Tony stood wearing only his slacks—and those not properly fastened. It was no wonder John and Brian began to grin and Kate and Lisa looked at her with wide eyes. The questions would start any minute, questions Olivia didn't know how to answer. All at once, her stomach turned over and she knew she was going to vomit.

She clapped a hand to her mouth and ran.

Behind her, she could hear Kate's gasp and John's muttered, "What the hell?"

But mostly what she heard was Tony saying in a bland tone, "She's all right. It's just morning sickness. Excuse me, will you?"

HE CAUGHT THE BATHROOM door before she could slam it in his face, then quietly locked it for her while she dropped to her knees in front of the toilet. He winced as she gagged, his sympathy extreme. When she sat back on her heels, he flushed the toilet, dampened a washcloth in cool water and handed it to her.

"Are you okay now?"

"Go away." She sounded weak and croaky and he sat down behind her and pulled her against his chest. Taking the washcloth from her hand, he wiped her face for her, then laid it aside.

"Aren't you supposed to take deep breaths or something?"

"That's during labor, you idiot."

Tony grinned at her acerbic tone, weak though it was. "Well, I haven't gotten around to reading all the books you've evidently gone through. Give me a little time, okay?"

She groaned again and he barely managed to get the toilet lid up for her. This time when she finished, she glared at him and demanded, "Go away and leave me alone."

"Don't be silly, Olivia. So you're sick? I've seen worse, I promise."

She staggered to her feet and went to the sink where she splashed water on her face. "Yeah. Worse is waiting in the other room, and you can be the one to explain."

"What's to explain? We're having a baby. They'd have found out sooner or later anyway."

"You know it's more than that and you could have spoken to them when I wasn't around!"

They could hear the rush of whispered voices from his family, and Tony shook his head. "There's no hope for it now." He opened the door and took her hand, but she held back. "Don't be a coward."

Olivia would have happily detoured into her bedroom and locked the door, but Tony didn't release her hand. He dragged her into the living room, where everyone had taken a seat, and said to the room at large, "We're having a baby."

Kate was the first to shoot from her seat, squealing in happiness. "Tony, this is so fantastic! When is the wedding?"

And without missing a beat, he said, "There won't be one."

Everyone stilled, their smiles frozen. And then the first volley of righteous umbrage hit. Of course he had to marry her. What could he be thinking of? Hadn't he enjoyed enough freedom of late? And babies deserved two parents. Kate even went so far as to put her arm around Olivia and remain protectively at her side while she glared daggers at him.

It was laughable, he thought. His family should know him better than this, but obviously they'd switched loyalties somewhere through this farce of a courtship. Then he shook his head. No, it was only that they thought they would save him from his own poor judgment. He wished them luck in their efforts.

And poor Olivia. He could see she was beginning to fret over the way they crucified him. Obviously they didn't realize it was Olivia who'd shied away from marriage, and if he told them the truth of the matter, it would really put her on the spot. He couldn't do it.

But Olivia could.

She looked around at all of them, dazed by their reactions. Brian was shaking his head and trying to be reasonable, Kate kept squeezing Olivia and patting her hand, and John was red in the face, telling Tony what a mistake he was making. Lisa, the only quiet one, stood twisting her hands together, the perfect picture of concern.

"Tony asked me to marry him!" She had to practically shout to be heard, and then the room went silent.

John was the first to react. "So what's the problem then?"

Olivia looked to Tony for help, but he just crossed his arms over his chest and waited. He was as curious as anyone to hear her explanation.

"It's not as simple as that."

"When has love ever been simple?"

Lisa again smacked John. "It's their business, John. Maybe we should just leave them alone."

"But Tony wants to marry her! And she obviously cares about him." He paused, then looked at Olivia. "You do, don't you?"

"I...yes."

"Just not enough to marry him?"

"It's complicated!"

John snorted. "How complicated can it be? You care about Tony. He's crazy about you. Hell, he's been so maudlin all week, I thought I'd have to shoot him to put him out of my misery," he joked.

Olivia's gaze shot to Tony's face, and he gave her a grim smile. "I have been a miserable bastard."

Tears welled in her eyes. "Oh, Tony."

She looked cornered, and he hated it. Enough was enough. He walked across the room and jerked the front door open. "Why don't you all get lost, all right? She's having a terrible time of it with this morning sickness stuff, and now she has all of you badgering her. Give us some time alone."

Lisa patted Olivia's arm. "The morning sickness will pass in a few weeks. And the rest of being pregnant is a breeze in comparison."

Kate gave her a firm hug. "I had it all day long, too. Try nibbling dry crackers as soon as your stomach acts up. And don't worry about the tears. Both Lisa and I cried all the time when we were carrying."

Brian squeezed her shoulder. "Hope you're feeling

better soon, hon. Try to make it for Christmas. Celebrating will take your mind off...other things."

Then only John was standing there, and Tony watched as he gave Olivia a stern look. "Whatever you think your reasons are, discuss them with him. Sometimes you find out the problems that worry you don't even exist." Then he gave her an affectionate kiss on the cheek and left.

The door closed with a resounding click, and the room was uncomfortably silent after that. For a moment, Tony didn't look at her. He kept his gaze on the door while he organized his thoughts. "You seemed surprised that I wasn't happy this past week."

Her response was trembling and uncertain. "I thought you'd still be too angry to be unhappy. Or if you were unhappy, I...well, was it because you thought I wouldn't involve you with the baby?"

Tony did turn to her then, and he made no effort to hide his anger. "The baby? I fell in love with you long before I knew you were carrying my baby. Hell, I think I may have been half in love with you for a long, long time. You were my first choice when I decided I wanted a baby. And then it didn't take me long to realize you were my *only* choice."

Her eyes were huge, her mouth open in a small "O." Tony shook his head, amused by her astonishment. How could she not have realized how much he cared for her?

"Olivia, we just made love, and it didn't have a damn thing to do with the baby."

"No?"

Stalking toward her, he smiled and said, "Nope. I get near you and I want you. I think about you and I want you. Hell, you throw up in a toilet and I want you."

"You do?"

He nodded, still coming closer. "And it's not just sex. I want to hold you, talk to you, listen to you laugh. God, I love watching you negotiate a deal."

She laughed at that and he finally reached her, but he didn't touch her. He lowered his voice and admitted, "It makes me hot as hell seeing you in your shark mode, being demanding and unrelenting. Of course, it was almost the same watching you give little Shawn his bottle. And when you defended me just now to my family—you do funny things to my insides, lady."

"You love me?"

"Hell, yes. Isn't that what I've been saying?"

"Oh, Tony." To his chagrin, she started to cry. When he reached for her, she stepped away. "There's so much you have to know."

He sat on the couch and propped his feet up. "Then don't you think it's time you told me?"

She nodded uncertainly, and he patted the couch beside him. When she started to sit there, he caught her and tugged her into his lap instead, holding her close and tucking her face into his shoulder. "All right. Now talk. And don't leave anything out."

She did. She told him about her trip to the hospital, that the pregnancy was still at risk, that there was a good chance she'd never get pregnant again. Even if she was able to carry this baby full-term, it might be their only child.

She didn't look at him as she spoke, choosing to keep her face hidden against him. Tony was relieved. It was damn difficult keeping his anger hidden, but he wanted her to finish the story, to make certain there were no more secrets between them. When she grew silent and he didn't immediately respond, she turned stiff in his arms.

"Tony?" He heard the uncertainty, the vulnerability, and his anger doubled. But he remained silent.

"You're angry?" she persisted.

"I'm furious." And he was.

She gave a small sob, but he didn't relent. "How could you do this, plan to go through all this alone, leave me in the dark? Didn't you think, somewhere along the line, I'd earned your trust? Have I ever given you any reason to believe I'm such a shallow ass that I'd let you go through this alone? Damn you, Olivia, are you ever going to open up to me?"

She had gone very still just after he started his tirade, and now she whispered, "I just did."

"What?" He was almost too angry to make sense of her words.

"I just opened up to you. And I do trust you. I swear. It's just that I love you so much, I didn't want you to be burdened with a wife who couldn't give you what you want."

"And if what I want most is you?"

She pushed away so she could see his face. Her dark eyes were liquid with tears, her cheeks blotchy, and he loved her so much, he wanted to cry with her. "Olivia, I love you."

She sniffed and threw herself against him, squeezing his neck so tightly he couldn't breathe. He choked out a laugh and said, "Marry me."

"But you want a baby, too."

"We're having a baby."

"But what if..."

"Shh." He laid his finger against her lips. "No what-ifs. I love you. You love me. If something happens, we'll have other children. And if you can't carry them, we'll adopt. It doesn't matter. What matters is that I need you with me."

Olivia laughed and squeezed him again. "I want you, too. And this baby. I'm being so careful, following all the doctor's orders, taking my progesterone twice a day..."

"You have to take pills?"

She slanted him a look. "Don't ask. Just understand that my body needs to absorb it now to help the baby. After the first trimester, the risks aren't nearly so high."

He loved holding her like this, seeing her so animated. "You've really studied up on this, haven't you?"

She ducked her head. "I've been so afraid."

He held her face, making her look at him. "From now on, you'll tell me. We'll get through it together."

Smiling, she said, "Yes."

"And you'll marry me."

It was his I'm-in-charge-now voice, and Olivia said, "Yes, sir."

He grinned. "You've just made my family very happy."

"And you?"

"I've just gotten everything I ever wanted. Of course I'm happy."

Two years later

"SHOULD WE TAKE the diaper bag on the plane with us?"

Tony laughed. "I wouldn't leave home without it." He walked into the bedroom where Olivia was packing. Her body once again slim and beautiful, though it wouldn't be that way for long. "How are you feeling?"

She turned and gave him and their thirteen month old son, Devon, a big smile. "Fine. Anxious."

"No morning sickness?"

"It's the strangest thing, but this time I feel wonderful."

"Lisa and Kate swore each pregnancy was different for them, as well."

Devon reached for his mother and Tony transferred him into her waiting arms. There was no hesitancy on her part now as she cuddled him close and kissed him and breathed his scent. Devon laughed and kicked his pudgy legs.

"Do you think he'll like flying? Maybe I should wait a little longer before making the Seattle trip."

"You've waited long enough. Besides, we'll only be there a week to look things over, and the woman you hired to manage the place is counting on seeing you. I have no doubt she's gone to great pains to impress you. And I did want to check in on the hotel anyway."

She laughed at him and shook her head. "You're worse than me. But running a business from across the country is easier than I'd thought it would be."

"With hotels, you have to adjust. Can't be everywhere at once."

"I know. And you taught me the secret long ago." She balanced Devon on her hip and went back to her packing. It sometimes amazed him the things she could now do one-handed. "As long as I hire good people, treat them well and expect the best from them, things, for the most part, run smoothly."

She bent to tuck a pair of shoes into the suitcase, and Tony couldn't stop himself from patting her rear. "Did I ever tell you how hot it makes me when you use that logical corporate tone?"

She cast him a look and said, "Why do you think I use it so often?"

"You always were a devious woman." He laughed when she playfully smacked him. Her earlier ploy was no longer a sensitive issue between them, especially since things had turned out so well. They had their baby, they had each other, and it was the best deal either of them had ever made.

This month's
irresistible novels from

Temptation ®

THE HEARTBREAKER by Vicki Lewis Thompson

Mike Tremayne had just seen beautiful Beth Nightingale for the first time in eight years and found her just as desirable as ever. But Beth had no intention of falling for Mike again; after all he'd already betrayed her twice, once when he became engaged to her sister, and then again, when he walked out on both of them.

SCANDALIZED! by Lori Foster

Blaze

Tony Austin wanted a baby, not a lover. So he asked Olivia Anderson to carry a baby for him. Little did he know that Olivia had no intention of getting pregnant but she liked the idea of a couple of nights of hot, *hot* sex with Tony! Then love got in the way and upset both their plans...

HIS DOUBLE, HER TROUBLE by Donna Sterling

The Wrong Bed

Brianna Devon had planned an intimate party for two as a surprise to celebrate Evan Rowland's return home. The surprise, however, was on her. Too late she discovered she was in bed *not* with her school sweetheart, but with his identical twin—her nemesis Jake Rowland! *And* she'd enjoyed every minute of it!

THAT WILDER MAN by Susan Liepitz

As teenagers, Max Wilder and his girlfriend Liza Jane had had a wild time—in town and in bed. Now a richer and a wiser man, Max had returned home. But he had no intention of giving her another chance to break his heart because, years ago, Liza Jane had run off and married his best friend...

Spoil yourself next month
with these four novels from

HOLD THAT GROOM! by Leandra Logan

Grooms on the Run

Bridal consultant Ellen Carroll had created the perfect wedding
for her best friend. But the bride had forgotten one small detail—
to ask the groom! Harry Masters was shocked and Ellen couldn't
blame him. Especially when she realised Harry was totally
wrong for her friend but totally right for her!

COURTING TROUBLE by Judith Arnold

Sophie Wallace and Gary Brett had better things to do than jury
duty. However, once they met each other in the courtroom, things
began to look up. Trouble was they were working on a case about
a bride suing her groom for jilting her. While Sophie had every
sympathy for the bride, Gary was siding with the groom!

HEART AND SOUL by Susan Worth

It Happened One Night

Kat Kylie and J.P. Harrington were both risk takers. But this time
Kat had lost a gamble and feared she stood to lose her
independence, too. After one night of steamy sex—she was
going to have a child who would rely on her. And a man who
would go to the ends of the earth to win her...

A HARD-HEARTED HERO by Pamela Burford

Tough ex-commando, Caleb Trent feared he was losing his edge
living in such close proximity with Elizabeth Lancaster. He'd
had no problem 'kidnapping' her out of a risky situation. But
keeping her captive was hard on his ego—and his libido.

On sale from 10th August 1998

MILLS & BOON®

COLLECTOR'S EDITION

Mills & Boon® are proud to bring back a collection of best-selling titles from Penny Jordan—one of the world's best-loved romance authors.

Each book is presented in beautifully matching volumes, with specially commissioned illustrations and presented as one precious collection.

Two titles every month at £3.10 each.

4 FREE

books and a surprise gift!

We would like to take this opportunity to thank you for reading this Mills & Boon® book by offering you the chance to take FOUR more specially selected titles from the Temptation® series absolutely FREE! We're also making this offer to introduce you to the benefits of the Reader Service™—

- ★ FREE home delivery
- ★ FREE gifts and competitions
- ★ FREE monthly newsletter
- ★ Books available before they're in the shops
- ★ Exclusive Reader Service discounts

Accepting these FREE books and gift places you under no obligation to buy, you may cancel at any time, even after receiving your free shipment. Simply complete your details below and return the entire page to the address below. *You don't even need a stamp!*

YES! Please send me 4 free Temptation books and a surprise gift. I understand that unless you hear from me, I will receive 4 superb new titles every month for just £2.30 each, postage and packing free. I am under no obligation to purchase any books and may cancel my subscription at any time. The free books and gift will be mine to keep in any case.

T8YE

Ms/Mrs/Miss/Mr...................................Initials ....
BLOCK CAPITALS PLEASE

Surname ....

Address ....

....Postcode....................................

Send this whole page to:
THE READER SERVICE, FREEPOST, CROYDON, CR9 3WZ
(Eire readers please send coupon to: P.O. BOX 4546, DUBLIN 24.)

Offer not valid to current Reader Service subscribers to this series. We reserve the right to refuse an application and applicants must be aged 18 years or over. Only one application per household. Terms and prices subject to change without notice. Offer expires 31st January 1999. You may be mailed with offers from other reputable companies as a result of this application. If you would prefer not to receive such offers, please tick box. ☐

Temptation is a registered trademark used under license.

The Sunday Times **bestselling author**

PENNY JORDAN

TO LOVE, HONOUR &

BETRAY

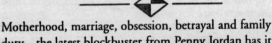

Motherhood, marriage, obsession, betrayal and family
duty... the latest blockbuster from Penny Jordan has it all.
Claudia and Garth's marriage is in real trouble when they
adopt a baby and Garth realises that the infant is his!

*"Women everywhere will find pieces of themselves in
Jordan's characters."*

—Publishers Weekly

MIRA

1-55166-396-1
AVAILABLE FROM JULY 1998